291

SUSAN MAY

ALSO BY SUSAN MAY

NOVELS

The Goodbye Giver (THE TROUBLES KEEPER 2)

(COMING LATE 2019)

Best Seller

The Troubles Keeper

Deadly Messengers

Back Again

NOVELLA

291

Behind the Fire

OMNIBUS

Happy Nightmares! Thriller Omnibus

SHORT STORY COLLECTIONS

Destination Dark Zone

(COMING JULY 2019)

Behind Dark Doors (one)

Behind Dark Doors (two)

Behind Dark Doors (three)

Behind Dark Doors (the complete collection)

(Includes one, two and three)

WHISPERSYNC AUDIBLE NARRATION

291

(COMING JUNE 2019)

Destination Dark Zone 2019

(COMING AUGUST 2019)

Best Seller

The Troubles Keeper

Deadly Messengers

Back Again

INTERNATIONAL BEST SELLING AUTHOR

SUSAN MAY

291

**Every road is the wrong road
when you're driving 291**

This was not the first-time that rookie cop Michael Chambers had found himself stuck in this broken-down police vehicle while the rain bucketed down outside.

In fact, this kind of 'bad luck' had happened almost every time he'd been assigned car 291. Usually, he'd get a flat, or the locks would jam or the damned onboard computer would freeze.

291, though, had a bloody and tragic history which might explain why this piece of metallic crap seemed so intent on driving him crazy— excuse the pun.

At first, he jokingly called it the demon car, but now he realized he may not be far off the truth. Something lurked inside this car and whatever it was, it meant him harm.

He was beginning to seriously believe that if he didn't fight back soon, this car might be the death of him. And he wasn't about to let that happen.

From international bestselling suspense author Susan May, comes a story of possession, desperation, and one man's battle against an unknown enemy. 291 is a brilliant short novel that will leave you breathless until the very last page and wondering what just happened?

⭐⭐⭐⭐⭐ "Probably the best Novella-length story I've read" Bill Schmidt

⭐⭐⭐⭐⭐ "Another great page-turner from the Mistress of the Twist." John Filar USA

⭐⭐⭐⭐⭐ "Could not put it down." Celia Marshall USA

⭐⭐⭐⭐⭐ "Pure Genius!" *Lisa Ensign USA*

DEDICATION

This story is dedicated to all those brave men and women who protect us from evil.

and to

my good friends
Peter and Diane Lynch

DEDICATION

I would rather be a little nobody, than an evil somebody

credited to Abraham Lincoln

NIGHT

"Well, fuck tonight!"

Police Officer Michael Chambers' voice echoed through the cruiser cabin.

"How can an onboard computer fail four times in a single month?" he asked nobody. "And always at night."

He smashed his palm against the steering wheel and swore again, louder this time because it hadn't helped the first time around, and now his hand hurt.

"Fuck! What'd I ever do to you?"

He'd only been out of the Academy for six weeks and had learned plenty of the truth. He'd learned that when you went in, they'd tell you shit about the real stuff while drilling into you to keep your wits highly tuned. Chambers understood this because he'd had enough jobs in his thirty-five years to understand the necessity of bullshit.

His first stop out of college—well, after quitting halfway through college—had been in a department store. They'd even managed to make *that* sound interesting during the induction. *You are here to serve and delight the customers in solving all their problems.* Yeah, right.

No matter what he sold them, some of those assholes weren't getting anything solved. After he'd grown tired of helping the me-me-

me set, he'd decided he didn't like people and he didn't like to study. So goodbye retail.

Then, he'd just fallen into becoming a security guard after a friend mentioned they were *always looking for guys*. Seemed the perfect choice. Fewer morons. Less standing on your feet, and plenty of reading time. Books, along with TV shows, were his thing.

He started as a bouncer in nightclubs. That was fun, until it wasn't. Drunks were nasty and the girls... all tease, no ease. After that, he did store security, then concerts and events, but he couldn't stand the crowds. And the noise.

The last six years, he'd been on patrol in a private gated community of rich assholes. He got to sit down—which the older he got, the more he appreciated—and enjoy his own fine company. It was the pinnacle of his search for the perfect employment.

He would have stayed doing the easy-as-you-please job for another twenty years too, but for his dad. That guy could shame a cat into chewing off its own paw. His dad, the decorated cop, and him, just a "babysitter in a uniform."

At least he had a job! If Carol hadn't up and left him—bitch took everything—and he hadn't been forced to move back home, maybe his father's jibes wouldn't have grated on him so much.

"Catch any stray dogs tonight?" Or, "How's those broken sprinkler reports?" Or the most annoying of all, "Get a good nap, Kiddo?"

His dad thought he was being funny, sorta. But Michael sensed the motive behind his words. He was ashamed of his son. If you weren't a cop, you were pretty much wasting your life. In the end, after six months of the never-ending repetition, he thought, *damn it! I'll show him.*

So here he was now, just graduated as a nearing middle-aged rookie with an already middle-body spread, when he was old enough to be the one calling the shots by his reckoning.

After all, he'd carried a gun as part of his job before and none of these pups could say that. Instead, he felt like a weary veteran as he observed that the sergeant must have a memory problem, since every sentence seemed to end in, "always be ready and alert."

He'd also just managed to survive another tedious-beyond-belief six weeks of the Field Training Officer, Pete Risotti.

The sole purpose of that idiot seemed to involve repeating what Michael already knew. After all, he wasn't a bright-eyed twenty-two-year-old. He knew how to conduct himself. The guy couldn't tell him enough times either, how lucky he was to enter the program *at his age*, thirty-five being the official age cut-off and Michael had been lucky to have the security experience that carried him into the force regardless.

Risotti had this annoying habit of staring across at him while he was trying to drive, which made Michael's neck and back bead with sweat. And worse, having distracted him already, Risotti would exclaim at nearly a shout, "Lack of focus can kill!"

This made him jump sometimes, and he so wanted to reply, *hell, other things can kill too. Like a punch to the head* or *repeating yourself ad nauseam... because you're boring me to fucking death.*

"Calls can come in thick and fast. Another patrol might need help. You have to make instant decisions, which sometimes represent life and death. Don't show up unprepared to put everything on the line. Be ready and alert, Chambers!"

The words *be ready and alert* circled in his head like one of those annoying pop songs that drove you mad. If he'd heard it once, he'd heard it fifty times. So, what made him, Mr. Listen-Up-I-Know-Every-thing, think that repetition to this degree was a great way to make him remember?

What a relief he'd felt when he was finally done with his probation. But things were about to get a whole lot worse and nobody had prepared him for that, had they?

On the first day solo, Michael showed up excited to pick up his patrol car and get out into the jungle. No more Risotti in his head, interrupting his thoughts and *sharing* his oh, so fascinating experiences.

Well, here's a tip for you, buddy: *those who can't do, teach.*

291. Yep. That was the car's number they gave him. Who would think that number would later come to haunt him? Fucking haunt him!

He'd turned up raring to go and yeah, yeah, ready for anything. But—as things turned out—nobody had given the speech to his cruiser. 291 wasn't ready for anything at all, except for driving him crazy.

Michael stayed alert alright, but not for action and not for danger. Instead, he was at the ready for whatever this damned piece of clanking shit could hurl at him. An almighty joke was going on and the punchline eluded him.

Each shift, when bad luck delivered him 291 as his vehicle again, something always went wrong.

The computer broke down all the time. Like *all* the time. Two punctures on good tires with plenty of remaining tread.

And what was with the internal light bulb flickering on and off at random moments as if some fucking ghost had taken control of the electronics? First time scared the shit out of him. Spooky as hell, because he thought he heard a voice too. His imagination probably but, damn, the way it surged bright and then switched on and off like Morse code was beyond weird.

Then, only yesterday, the trunk jammed open about three inches wide. He'd had to throw so much weight on it to get the thing down and locked, that he'd gone and left a dent in the lid. Well, served the bitch right for causing him grief for no good reason.

Thank God for being assigned a quiet zone. Whether because he was a rookie or due to his family legacy, at least he wasn't fighting dangerous criminals as well as a renegade car.

He was such a cliché. Father a cop. Grandfather a cop. His older brother too, though Bill had moved to a different city. Smart guy. Get away from the nagging parents and the constant, "So you're Joe Chambers' son? Great guy and excellent cop."

Maybe that was why he'd fought the cop-as-a-career choice for so long, because he'd somehow known he'd have to endure the accolades for his dad.

Now he was *one of them*.

Michael had imagined the boys of the family sitting around the Sunday dinner table swapping stories of *The Jungle,* as his dad had called the job. "I'm off to hunt the animals," had been his catch-phrase when walking out the door. "When you grow up, you can come hunting with me," he'd said to his fascinated sons.

Life was funny though. By the time they'd aged enough to appreciate their father's occupation, his dad didn't seem to want to share war tales anymore.

"I've seen too much. No need to upset your mother with it." When pressed by his eager boys to share more exciting stories like he used to do, he'd reply, "A job's a job. That's it. Nothing to see here." He'd laugh but there was something lying hidden there, like a crab in a hole.

After his retirement three years ago, his old man's reticence had his son's imagination seeking out the reasons for his secretiveness. He'd imagined all kinds of nightmare experiences, and that was why he couldn't find the words. Now he'd joined the force, he knew the reasons. There was a lot of paperwork and a lot of bullshit and not much excitement.

The man who'd grown reticent in sharing his work life still had enough enthusiasm left for the wayward son made good. He wore the widest smile on Michael's Academy graduation day, but what he seemed to enjoy even more was the back-slapping from his colleagues. He'd donated another spawn to the cause as if he and Bill were little toy soldiers in some strategy game.

Instead of keeping it all to himself, his dad could have warned him that reality would never meet expectations. While his parents liked game shows and Westerns—his mom sitting there knitting alongside his father, *to keep him company*—he darn well knew Michael loved police shows, knew that he devoured them and had done so since he was a kid.

Law & Order. The Wire. NCIS. Narcos. CSI. He loved them all. He thought *Dexter* and the *Sopranos* too improbable, but did enjoy imagining what he would have done differently to catch a serial killer or bring down the mob.

Everything happened within an hour. Crimes were committed, clues left behind, and all sorts of fun was had as partners worked their way through the deviously elusive little details. The female detectives were always cute, sassy and tough. He wanted a girl like that one day. Not someone who sat watching shows just because her husband liked them.

So, he could have given him a big heads-up that cop work wasn't much of a step-up from security in the action stakes. Car chases, foot pursuits, intense interrogations and camaraderie with the guys had been notable in their absence, even from day one at the academy. He put it down to his age and being a tad overweight. The younger generation, with all their Instagram and Snapchat, was so judgmental. And he got it! He was a little judgy himself.

For a start, he hadn't even been assigned a partner. What was up with that? They only partnered you up if you patrolled dangerous zones, such as the areas with their high gang activity and impossible crime rates. He hypothesized his boss viewed him as still on his training wheels and so he got the dullsville suburbs. Nothing happened, well nothing major.

Yes, okay, on occasion, you'd get slammed, calls exploding from the radio in rapid fire. Domestics, speeding, jaywalking tickets, plenty of checking on old people when a relative unable to contact them turned up panicked. The monotony of the *same events, different faces* had him yawning within the first few weeks.

Unlike in his previous employment, he couldn't while away the time reading, and so it was boring at times. And his tolerance for boredom was low to non-existent. And that was fair enough because nobody had warned him about that. In fact, quite the opposite, because they all kept telling him to be prepared. What exactly was he preparing for? Falling asleep?

He wanted to solve murders and bank robberies and kidnappings and outsmart wily criminals. Call him naïve, but he hadn't realized until he patrolled the streets for real, that he didn't give a damn about the people. He didn't hate the public but didn't rate them much either.

He was never going to be a corrupt cop like Denzel Washington in *Training Day* or Matt Damon in *The Departed* for one good reason. He wasn't stupid. None of the dirty cops survived in those films and he took that as a moral warning.

But really! The whole thing was a farce. *Serve and protect* for the pittance of a wage they paid?

Forget it. He deserved so much more. Precisely what he deserved, he was unsure. This career move was looking like a big fat mistake already. His work associates weren't buddy-like, and the job was a crushing, mind-numbing bore. The worst part of this, though, was that he had nobody with whom to share his latest suspicions. If he shared what he had begun to suspect, he'd be thought of as crazy. Heck, he even thought he might be losing it.

But it was 291, this fucking asshole of a car.

He'd begun to think, maybe—and yeah, it did sound bat-shit ridiculous—that this metal-box motherfucker had it in for him. A demon possession was happening, and that was where his mind kept traveling, and it wasn't just that. No.

Every time the thoughts entered his mind, he'd pushed them away, but they'd come straight back. Something kept whispering that he wasn't losing his marbles, that 291 was not just a car but harbored some kind of malevolent force.

It was out to do something terrible to him, and he couldn't figure out why.

RAIN

When his dad had once talked about life as a cop, he sure hadn't mentioned any of the mundane stuff Michael was having to deal with today. Like helping old ladies find their missing dogs.

Incidents: three.

Then there was the question of how many tickets he'd written out in a single hour for traffic violations: that was nine so far.

And finally, there'd been that stinking bullshit the likes of which Michael had faced an hour ago between two neighbors. Like three-year-olds in a playground, that's how they'd behaved.

One argued that the other had swapped their trash cans. Shitty, stinking cans, for Christ's sake! The big-nosed asshole, who yelled like they were discussing a murder, claimed *his* now *"smelled worse"* than the other one. He should have just let them kill each other and done the world a gigantic favor. Jesus, he'd willingly give them each a knife to do it with.

291 had certainly tipped his thinking over tonight.

And decisions needed making.

Every time the twit at the garage assigned him the car—which seemed way more than could possibly be legitimate—the automobile poked and prodded at him. At least, that was how it felt.

He stared out through the windshield at the dismal weather, his hand throbbing from the whack he'd delivered the steering wheel.

Man, why'd I go do a dumb thing like that? he thought, pressing his fingers into his palm to ease the pain.

His mind was wandering, he decided, when he caught himself admiring each raindrop's trail as *perfection* as it slithered down the glass. The car sure picked its moments. Perfect timing to scramble his computer, with the heavens sending a flood that'd terrify Noah.

To fix the piece of crap, the protocol was to find somewhere safe nearby to stop. So that was the reason he now found himself parked behind Gordon's Garage. Though the display screen was inside, the processing unit lay in the trunk. God knew why! What half-wit had thought of that design feature?

The minute he'd stopped and turned off the engine, the rain arrived. If he'd anticipated the storm's severity, he'd instead have chosen a fire station or somewhere undercover.

He craned his neck to look up through the windshield, trying to gauge if it would pass soon. Two seconds out there and he'd be a sad, wet puppy for the rest of the shift. Driving to another venue was an option, but he'd already radioed his position when reporting the breakdown. He didn't want to have to call again and explain, *boo hoo, I don't want to get wet* like he was some girl.

No, the best plan by far was to sit tight until the weather eased. This would give him a chance to also chew through what had become pressing life choices.

If he quit—and this latest event had him leaning that way—what would his parents say?

Wait; even before that little scenario, he would first suffer the *resignation* discussion with the Sergeant. An interesting chat, for sure. A Cheshire Cat smile spread across his face as the conversation played out in his mind.

"Sorry, I'm bored. And your fucking car is a monster. You can take your job and ram it up your—"

Yeah, that'd work out so peachy! They'd no doubt suggest a psych test.

Good luck then in getting any kind of employment, with a mental issue plastered all over your résumé.

He'd be considered a deserter too, after the police force's time investment in him. It was all about money, wasn't it? Never about the little guy and his needs.

He could always become an *Uber* driver or pizza delivery slave.

Yay, so awesome, Mike. Way to go.

That'd bring him back to sitting in a car for hours, delivering high-carb, high-fat mush to fat, lazy executive types or ignorant moms who couldn't be bothered feeding their kids right. Nope, not happening. After 291, cars were off his list of most desirable possessions.

He checked out through the windshield again. A weak moon shone in the distance through a break in the thick clouds, as if ashamed. He was no weather jock, but the storm didn't look like stopping anytime soon. His shift ended in ninety minutes and he had no intention of working another minute longer than paid.

This left little choice but to get out, run to the rear, pop the trunk, and then endure a drenching while he flicked the reboot switch. The hard drive needed time to stop. So, he'd be the unfortunate one standing in a storm waiting for the precious darling to do its thing.

Please, too, while out there freezing your balls off and catching pneumonia, Officer Chambers, always remain alert.

That fucking thought again!

Yeah, sure, I'll be on my best behavior, even if my useless equipment isn't.

He checked the lot perimeter twice. The only entrance, a short driveway to the side, prevented any surprises. Security lighting—which annoyingly switched on every minute thanks to the wind—illuminated his isolation. The eerie surrounds had him imagining worse things than criminals. He saw imaginary *Walking Dead* zombies beating on his windshield, blood dripping from their gawping mouths, and shriveled hands smashing the glass. Yuk! He hated that show. So unrealistic.

Several empty cars parked at careless angles surrounded him and

291. They were most likely waiting for their owners' pick-up after repairs or were booked in for the next day. Still, he watched each one for several minutes, looking for any movement.

Always be alert, Officer Chambers. Always be aware of your surroundings and unexpected danger.

The increasing volume of the cascading rain on the roof reminded him it was probably best to accept he'd be getting wet; he should really just get this done pronto.

Okay, let's do this.

Chambers glanced in his rear-view and side mirrors, for no reason except it made him feel more detective-y, if that was a word. *Probably not.* He leaned forward, snaked his hand below the dash and popped the trunk. Then he reached across himself to pull on the handle, shoving his shoulder into the door's panel. As it swung open, a creaky hinge groaned a complaint.

"Yep, imagine how I feel," he replied.

Cold, damp air rushed inside and pushed at him as he climbed out into the night, stepping into a deep puddle, which instantly soaked his socks and shoes.

God, Jesus, Mary and Joseph, this is hellish!

His arm came up and over his head in a futile attempt at cover—for what little good it did—as he shimmied along the car's side. He got that trunk up in one second flat and bent his body into the opening to flick the on-off switch to off.

Ten seconds they'd told him he must stand there, waiting, while the screwed-up thing turned off and slowed to a stop.

How he hated pandering to its preciousness.

Always speak in hushed and respectful tones. Never look on in disrespect, and for fuckety-fuck's sake, never curse nearby or let it sense your fear. Yeah, yeah. And count to ten if you must reboot or you might damage the delicate ghost in the machine.

Well, he'd love to exact his own damage. A tire iron sprung to mind. He felt his biceps flexing at the mere thought of swinging it.

Five assholes. Six assholes. Seven assholes. Eight assholes. Nine assholes. Ten, shit-for-nothing, assholes!

There! Done!

Chambers flipped the switch and leaned in farther. His ear was within an inch of the unit in order to listen for the whirr of the hard-drive. He wasn't getting back out of the car again if this didn't work.

Once he heard the *zzah-zzah-zzah* repeat for a few seconds, he slammed the trunk and crouch-ran to his door. His hand fumbled with the handle before gaining a grip and yanking it open.

What seemed like an hour later, he flopped into his seat, smacking his knee against the lower end of the steering wheel as he did. For a brilliant moment, a sharp jolt traveled through his leg and then was gone.

"Fuck you!"

He swallowed a deep breath of cool air to calm himself. When he exhaled, he let out a huge burp and spoke through it.

"Take that."

The words exploded in the cabin, sounding like a cross between a fart, a growl, and monster-speak. Honest to God, this was bullshit. He was wet to the bone and his shoes had tightened like they'd become screw-turning torture mechanisms. And he couldn't even see out for *heightened awareness* or entertainment; the inside of the windshield was wetter than the outside, condensation now running down to form pools on the dash. He felt sure his body was steaming.

His attention turned now to the computer screen as it awoke and grew brighter. Several lines of code spilled across the gray-blue background. Experience told him he must wait forty-five seconds. If it didn't reset, he'd get to do it all over again. Yay, for him.

"Come on. Come on," he whispered, nodding his head, hoping positive thoughts might help where technology invariably failed.

If he couldn't make it work, then he'd need to document everything manual-style. *Pen and paper, baby.* Then, back at the precinct, it'd mean an hour of data input. Such a waste of time. *His* time, for which they wouldn't even pay him.

The alternative was to return to Headquarters for another car, kept for emergency rotation. Those were worn out, ready for retirement, dogs with engines, which he imagined was 291's problem. So, he might end up in the same situation and gain nothing. Better the devil you know, he figured. *Devil* being the operative word.

Now he was wet, hungry and his stomach burned. The stress felt as if weevils squirmed and burrowed inside his intestines.

A few more seconds, maybe twelve, fifteen more *assholes*, and he'd know. He breathed deep, long mouthfuls of the damp air to settle himself. This could take a while. Last time, it was three reboots before the computer worked, which was fine if the weather wasn't raining down rabid German Shepherds and screaming cougars.

Ping. Ping-Ping. Ping.

The program lit up on the ten-inch screen and awaited his command.

Hallelujah! He pulled it to face him straight on and tapped the keyboard. His preference was to punch it, but instead, he studied the inputted name. *John McAsshole* appeared in the search space. That was the name he called every perp in his mind.

Yup, everything seemed fine and dandy.

He hit the back button to delete the fictitious name, although curiosity tempted him to run it. Imagine having that surname?

Do you take this man, Johnny McAsshole, to be your lawful wedded husband?

At least that thought brought a small smile to his face. God, he was a funny guy!

Okay, all operational; now to work. Not that he expected excitement to be looming on the horizon with this godawful weather. Criminals liked being drenched about as much as cops. Crimes of significance rarely happened in the rain, they'd told them at the Academy.

He turned the key to start the car, pleased with himself that he'd kept his cool. His anger could manifest at times far worse than the act of slamming a steering wheel. He'd worked on that for a while. Swearing and bitching helped. It released the tension in his system until the next shit storm blew up.

A rapid-fire *click-click-click-click-click-click-click-click* filled the car's cabin.

He turned the key again.

Click-click-click-click-click-click-click-click-click.

"Aww, crap."

Chambers slumped back in the seat ready to smack the wheel again, but he knew better now. Instead, he reached for the mic, keyed it on. "Fucking, shitting, pissing crap," he said. "That's all I gotta say." He inhaled deeply, composing himself.

"Two-nine-one to Headquarters."

A female operator's voice replied, "Headquarters, two-nine-one, go ahead."

"Two-nine-one, Headquarters. Enjoying a hell of a night."

"Headquarters, two-nine-one, say again."

I said, what a fucking night, and I quit.

That was what he dearly wanted to say but they recorded every-thing. With the *#metoo* movement, who knew if the operator might take offense. Everybody took offense these days at every fucking thing.

"Two-nine-one, Headquarters. Car is dead. I repeat, I have a flat battery. I'm stuck here behind Gordon's Garage on El Camino."

"Headquarters, two-nine-one. Got that. I'll get someone out to you as soon as possible. With this weather, we're really behind. Might be an hour or so. Sit tight."

Shit! Shit! Shit!

"Two-nine-one, Headquarters. Acknowledged."

He keyed off the mic with a sharp, annoyed flick, then stared out of his side window. The raindrops drizzled downward, slipping and sliding and having a hell of a time at his expense.

Chambers inhaled through his nose and exhaled through his mouth. He leaned back and closed his eyes, imagining he was anywhere but here in this car, the car that hated his very bones. The feeling was mutual; he hated the cursed, demon-possessed, mechan-ical albatross which made his job so much harder. The job he'd also begun to hate.

Hate. Hate. Hate.

Yeah, it sure had been a great fucking night!

And the worst thing about it was, he knew there'd be nothing better on another shift, on any other night in car 291.

COCKTAILS

2012 PART 1

Frank Chester kissed his wife Lucy's cheek, told her he loved her—and he meant it—and headed out the door. He would report to the precinct for a Monday briefing, then grab a car and take off for his rounds. With the overtime scheduled for him, that would make it eleven, twelve hours before he'd be home.

Today would be the same as any other, except for one detail. He'd be submitting his vacation request. Nineteen months had passed since his last break. They were understaffed, with overtime on offer. Whenever he and Lucy discussed getting away, the guilt at abandoning his post and his co-workers nipped at his conscience. Lying on a beach sipping cocktails—her preference—instead of relaxing in the wilderness, fishing and sitting by a cabin fire sipping a beer—his preference—just didn't appeal.

Then last week, the boss had mentioned his accrued leave and that the higher-up pencil-pushers directed all overdue time needed to be used by the year's end. So, he'd had no choice, guilt or not.

Frank was on the eleven-until-seven morning shift, but he arrived at ten to fill out the forms. That took a few minutes, and afterward, he checked in with his sergeant to confirm it was all good. Then he headed to the roll call, where he enjoyed the usual banter with the guys before the briefing began. Sheesh, he loved these boys. He found a camaraderie with them, something he'd never experienced with his civilian friends.

Today, the Supervisor advised there were no major incidents outstanding. An organized breaking-and-entering group had hit homes on the south side. They'd catch them soon enough since they had been so brazen as to commit most in broad daylight.

Then, some creep had been exposing himself within walking distance of a school, while a lone vandal had broken windows of businesses in the river precinct. And last, there came the usual: an elderly man suffering dementia, missing since around ten the previous night.

So, should be a good shift ahead if his luck held. He'd prefer not to be on the lookout for a murderer or rapist. He hated those. In his twelve years on the job, he'd never gotten over innocent people getting killed for a few dollars, or violence over something inconsequential. He didn't have kids. So, while he hated pedophiles, he didn't harbor the abject horror of a parent in those circumstances, but anyone assaulting a woman was still about as low as they came, to his mind.

He walked with a group of fellow officers to the garage to pick up his car. Turned out a few of the guys had also put in for leave today. They jokingly discussed taking a trip together, and while Frank agreed that would be the best use of their vacation, he didn't mean it. He'd rather be with Lucy, even on some goddamned beach, sweating his nuts off and bored as hell. And besides, he wouldn't live to enjoy that time with the guys if he dared suggest such a thing to her.

As he walked toward his cruiser, a hint of excitement at the thought of the vacation buoyed his mood even more. Now, all he needed to do was convince Lucy how wonderful she'd find the mountain air. He'd already researched a place. *Little Fork.* He'd read the information so many times that he knew it by memory.

Escape to a summer cottage in Little Fork and you will enjoy all the ingredients you need for a relaxing lake vacation. Whether you spend the day picking wild berries, exploring old logging trails or fishing the bountiful waters, you can count on enjoying laidback evenings by your rental's fire pit. Nearby are cozy, quality eateries if the fish ain't biting.

His wife loved a good meal. That might just tip her over to his way of thinking. Lying on a beach with this belly of his—grown with so little effort over the last five years—just didn't do it for him. He was a beer guy, not a cocktail or wine sipper.

Frank climbed into 291, furnished the passenger seat with his belongings—a lunch Lucy made, his phone and the latest John Grisham novel—and drove out into the sunshine. By the time he returned, it'd be dark, and he'd be exhausted.

No partner for him again today. You didn't need one in low-crime areas. And he liked low-crime areas. Not saying there wasn't excitement occasionally but getting to know nice people in his patrol rounds made work satisfying. These were good folk he protected, and he took that job seriously. They counted on him to ensure their suburb stayed just as peaceful as always.

Drummed into him was the public relations part of the job, easily done because his parents had raised him to be community-minded. Not to mention Lucy and her *mind your manners out there* quips. That woman was more insistent than the Sergeant.

She needn't have bothered because four sisters give you plenty of female perspective. If you don't catch on quick enough as a defenseless kid, you die. Or wish you had.

He chuckled at the thought.

It had done him good though to have them on his case and he remained close to his sisters, even now. They were great people and he adored his nephews and nieces.

Perspective. That was what came from a solid upbringing and having good human beings in your life; instead of becoming annoyed by mundanity and the unpopular hours involved in his job, he looked at the positives.

Like the time he'd been sent to a breaking-and-entering and it turned out to be what he labeled *the possum heist*. The *victim* was the sweetest little old lady—think Betty White's *Golden Girls'* character, Rose. Her garden backed on to a wooded reserve and an adult possum had somehow gotten itself inside for shelter during a storm. Frank discovered the creature holed up in the spare room, scared witless. Took some wrangling to steer it outside. But he managed. You worked out stuff with this job, that's for sure. He was now convinced he could take any possum into custody unaided.

Meantime, the wind had brought down a branch big enough to be a whole tree on its own right there in little ol' Rose's driveway, blocking her car in the garage. She was near in tears telling him how she couldn't afford to have it cleared.

So, Frank had rounded up a few of the guys to return the next day and move it for her. They even scored their ugly mugs in the local paper for their trouble.

The image of the diminutive, gray-haired woman standing amid six uniformed men was reminiscent of a Ma Barker photograph. The boys stood there grinning, each holding a teacup and a slice of cake. Yeah, they were tough cops and had the photo to prove it. Hell, some were so tough they even drank the tea, though they were strictly coffee guys.

Frank sometimes cruised past Miss Rose's house and, when he wasn't busy, he'd drop in to check on her. Maybe he'd do that after this shift, if only because the sky was threatening rain again, coloring everything a paler shade of dull.

"Plenty of sunshine in Florida," his wife had chirped this morning when he'd peered outside through the floral lace curtains. *Bless the woman.* She'd sewn those curtains herself, and he didn't have the heart to tell her they hung a fraction uneven and crooked. One just skimmed the top of the carpet, while the other looked like a trouser leg at half-mast. She didn't seem to notice.

"Is there now?" he'd replied. "But there's also a bunch of Floridians, so that cancels it out."

She had punched his arm playfully. "Shut it, Mr. Chester, and get outta here. I got better things to do than listen to you and your silly jokes."

The radio was busy from shift start and continued well into the afternoon. His first call was a domestic dispute at eleven-thirty. People needed to stop drinking so much.

Then, a kid was reported missing after he hadn't arrived at school; the parents had no clue to his whereabouts. It took Frank forty minutes to find him at the mall. The mom grabbed the boy's arm upon his return and yanked him inside. He'd learn more in the next hour than anything he'd missed in class. Rule Number One: don't piss off the female of the house.

At four, it was time for a late lunch by Walton Park on Third and Bennett Streets, providing a welcome break. He'd been thinking about Lucy's pastrami sandwich the entire day. She had a way with mayonnaise that grew his love for her with every bite. It just made everything zing in his mouth.

This park was a quiet gem of a haven, and with the overcast light deepening the green of the grass and trees, it seemed as if nature used a camera filter. As he chewed on his delicious delight, he saw himself sitting under one of those trees with a book. Except, he transposed the scene to the side of a lake at Little Fork. Add a fishing rod and a couple of beers, and, yeah, you had heaven right there. He could doze off in that very spot, imagining the warmth of the sun and the weight of the book lying open on his chest, the cover toward the cloudless sky.

But reality swung him back to the job and fifteen minutes later, he was well into his afternoon filled with issuing speeding tickets, jay-walking cautions and attending two minor car accidents. He didn't mind that today was a slow one. All this vacation thinking had filled his body with a mild case of lethargy.

When the call came in at 8:14 PM, he'd been on duty for nine hours, fourteen minutes and he was feeling tired. Only forty-six minutes until end-of-shift time, and it couldn't come soon enough.

Thank God, this call was just a vandalized corner café in a quiet, suburban street, one of those restored buildings that had once housed a local store. Every three blocks had had one before cars and superstores came along, forever changing the meaning of *local*. He remembered one from his youth, a store run by Mr. Cadee and his wife, but kids these days would only know soulless malls, and more was the pity, Frank thought.

When he keyed the mic ready to respond, he paused. It occurred to him to let it go because it could take him beyond the end of his shift. But that wasn't him. And it sure wasn't the husband of one Lucy Chester. You did the right thing and the right things would come to you. That's what his woman always said but she did have the luxury of not seeing the things he'd seen on the job. Right didn't always bring right.

He told himself it wouldn't take too long, sighed and shook his head as he responded.

"Two-nine-one to headquarters, I'm three blocks from reported premises location—"

Five minutes later, Frank was cruising down Vanguard Road at ten miles an hour, checking the darkened streetscape as he neared the corner location of the café. He traveled past the bright blue building with the word *Delish* painted across a window and a sign attached above the door. Another window showed a coffee cup and a pie with steam rising from it. *Best apple pie this side of the river!* was painted below the image.

As Frank slowed, he shone a flashlight over the façade and all looked fine until he turned the corner. On this side, broken glass lay scattered on the pavement, glittering in the illumination. He doubted they'd gotten inside because—behind the shattered window—iron security grilles were affixed, of the type you had to slide across.

Silly kids indulging in tomfoolery, no doubt.

Fresh graffiti lay scrawled below the window grilles, but he didn't recognize the markings, the tags being individual or gang symbols. The only way to combat these was to remove them but more invariably sprouted like weeds, so Frank always figured this old chestnut just didn't hold water.

He circled the block again, checking for any other damage to properties, or for movement. But except for the window, all seemed peaceful. Frank slowly pulled over to the curb several houses away from the business. If the perpetrator was still lingering nearby, Frank might stand a small chance of being surprised by him—or of surprising the guy himself. His years of experience had informed him that things usually went a lot better when you didn't announce your arrival with sirens blaring.

The windows of surrounding homes glowed a bright yellow as their occupants settled in for the night. That tugged at him, thinking of Lucy waiting at home, and of his anticipation of a pleasant late-night meal and a hot chocolate while they caught a TV show. He didn't much care what they watched, he simply enjoyed relaxing into his easy chair and letting the day drain from his mind and body.

The suburb surrounding Delish was one of older families with kids in high school or just graduated, but still living at home. Neat streets and cordial residents made this a desirable ZIP Code. Domestic disputes or arguing neighbors' calls were rare, so he had no reason to be on hyper alert. *Just kids* crossed his mind again.

As Frank turned the key to kill the engine, he reached up to touch the Saint Christopher medal hanging from the rearview mirror. It was a gift from his wife, a practicing Catholic. Him? He could take it or leave it. But the woman didn't ask for much, so he'd converted, if not in his heart, at least in his head.

Pushing open the door, he exited, surveilling the street as he did, to check for sudden movement. You could tap as many religious medals as you wanted but one momentary lapse of concentration was to tempt fate. But he sure felt tired and really wasn't going to do more than document this; then, forensics could come out, when and if they got to it, to check for fingerprints.

He passed several houses, shining his flashlight into their pristine yards, before reaching the building. He peered inside the darkened building, held his light to the window and waved it across the interior. Everything seemed to be in order. No upturned chairs or tables and no sign of entry. Sure looked like a nice little place to add to the charm and sense of community of the surrounding streets.

Luckily, other than the shattered window, they appeared to have had no other loss. He wondered why the culprits had even bothered with this place, with no access available. Just outright vandalism by little I-don't-give-a-shit troublemakers.

Turning left, he rounded the storefront and shone his flashlight up the brick-wall facing the street. His gaze traveled over the pavement and surrounds, looking for clues to the culprit. Or culprits. These little creatures traveled in packs.

Nothing obvious that he could see.

He noted the lack of a security camera, which would make the prospect of finding the vandals difficult, if not impossible. Even though he knew the answer to the question of why do damage for damage's sake, it always crossed his mind. There were so many reasons and none of them made much sense to law-abiding folk.

His cautious nature caused him to remain on high alert, but he relaxed a little as his expectations of discovering anyone still in the vicinity diminished with every moment.

"Ran home to Mama, didn't you?" he muttered. "Catch ya next time, you rats."

Ten yards along, at the end of the building, he came upon a back lane; not unusual in older areas. Eighty years ago, these were dirt service roads for deliveries and trash collection. Now, they supplied rear car parking access. Unlike the neighborhood streets, the only lighting here was thanks to the moon.

He peered down the alley but fifteen yards in, where the arc of the street lights couldn't reach, the vista melted into dark shadows and gray-black nothingness.

He raised his arm and held the flashlight aloft to illuminate the long stretch. It appeared clear with no movement, the symmetry of the lane broken only by a mound of what appeared to be wood or metal near the midway point.

Frank checked his watch. Aww, sheesh, in five minutes his shift ended.

Did I really need to bother with this?

Then he thought of the dismay felt by the victims of such senseless crimes, and he decided that, since he was here, the two minutes to check it out wouldn't exactly kill him.

Frank sidestepped his way forward, crisscrossing foot over foot as he went, his body swiveling left to right. Moving this way, he could scan 180 degrees. Nobody was surprising him, not even a cat.

Look left. Rear. Forward. Right. Rear. Repeat.

He'd traveled halfway when he heard a noise. The sound was faint and on the periphery of his hearing, but he thought it might have been a stifled sneeze or a cough. Or maybe not.

Maybe it was just a dog or a cat, but it was enough to halt his progress and cause him to make a slow rotation, so he now faced back toward the entrance. He held his breath and stood statue-like, cocking his head, listening.

When he'd run out of breath, he exhaled a steady release of air but heard no further noise. He stayed there, though, for a long minute because he sensed something in the air. Something not right. Out of balance. After this long on the job, a man learned to trust his gut.

His hand moved to his holstered gun—not rapidly, just a gentle sliding of a palm—as he made a slow 360-degree turn. He was aware his arms had grown rigid and his legs stiff. Even though it was nothing, he felt the rise of his heartbeat. You couldn't stop adrenaline no matter how much you trained your mind.

The flashlight's glow swept across the ramshackle row of property boundaries. Wooden fences attached to brick, concrete or patterned metal in no particular order or design, ran the length of the lane.

There seemed nowhere for someone to hide. Each segment of fence wore a gate, though. Perhaps that was where his little vandals had scampered? He'd clip their ears if he found them for making him work overtime on his overtime.

Left to right, right to left, he swung his light, straining to see detail in the dark void. Again, he held his breath as he squinted to see and cocked his head to the side to listen.

Someone was there. Yes, they were. Whether they were a property owner or the perp or perps, he couldn't say.

The wind picked up, the barest whisper brushing across his cheek and forehead. It felt cold and he shivered. He must be getting old. Normally, he didn't feel the cold. Heat, yes, but it'd have to be mid-winter before he'd start wearing a jacket.

No sound anywhere, so he changed his mind and decided what he'd heard was a branch scraping against a window or flicking a wall. His imagination was having a right fun time at his expense. Wouldn't be the first time lately, either. Lucy was spot-on, as always; he needed a vacation more than he cared to admit. Even as another shiver shook him thanks to the cool night air, his thoughts traveled to a warm beach somewhere.

Damn, that woman's persuasive arguments were actually winning him over. Right about now, lying there in the sun sounded like heaven.

Forget hiking in the hills, wearing heavy jackets and checking yourself for ticks as you examined the brush scratches on your calves and forearms. "Let's have a real vacation, Lucy," he saw himself saying as he walked in their front door an hour later.

Piña colada on a white sandy beach. Yeah, if that's what she wanted then, baby, that's what he'd give her. She had always held down their fort. And every time he left for a shift, he knew she worried until she heard his key in the door. Though she never said the words, she didn't have to because he saw it in her eyes.

Foolish woman. No way was he not coming home to his girl.

STONES

2012 PART 2

Frank smiled as he lowered his flashlight, turned back down the darkened lane and continued onward. He'd be late for his handover meetup at this rate, so he needed to move. He'd ensure it was clear and then report that the kids—or whoever had decided breaking a window was the best use of their time—had gotten away.

Ten steps later and the hairs on the back of his neck stood up. Don't ever ask a cop how they knew something was about to happen. They just always knew, like bad intent had a frequency into which they learned to tune their minds.

He wasn't alone in that, either. He was sure of that, just like he knew without a doubt he'd miscalculated coming down here without calling for backup—or not even coming down here at all.

And it wasn't just the squeak of a hinge echoing high and loud from the row of fences he'd just checked. It was the sense of danger descending upon him, a dark, oppressive cloak warning him like an evacuation alarm blaring from the heavens.

In his mind's eye, he saw the gate, five, six houses back, hanging half open. The easy access to the property behind had registered with him, but he'd figured it was a careless homeowner, and nothing more.

Slowly, he turned his head in the sound's direction. His body then followed the rotation as if he was sneaking around a corner; his feet shuffled only an inch with each step, whisper-quiet.

He kept the flashlight by his side, thinking this would give the illusion to whoever was there that he hadn't sensed their presence. His eyes squinted into the dark, but though he felt someone there, he detected no movement, no further sound either.

He lifted his arm and slipped his fingers near-silently over his holster, fumbling with the lock to free his gun. They were smart little critters these ones—or this one—waiting for him to walk past. Well, they'd find themselves disappointed because he'd become convinced it was kids. Stupid fools had picked the wrong cop tonight. He was a good rat-catcher because he possessed patience.

Frank saw himself as he sat down to a late dinner and a glass of wine with Lucy, telling her what a wily man she'd married. Then maybe there'd be teasing about the beach vacation before he'd reveal his change of heart. Afterward, he'd suggest they practice what could happen while relaxed, suntanned and filled to bursting with exotic food. She would give that beautiful, husky laugh of hers, playfully slap him and—

The thing flew out of the dark.

No time to duck.

A cat?

No, a bird?

A bat maybe?

His stomach clenched. He despised bats.

Whatever it was, the thing had flown right past him.

A smacking thud.

His gaze followed to where it landed.

The wooden fence, just over his left shoulder.

Not a bullet or a knife. Bigger. Much bigger.

Not a bat, thank God!

How he really hated the nasty, flea-bitten little creatures. He'd helped check an attic in his first month on the job and disturbed at least five of them up there. They all flew at him like black mini-missiles. Eek, he could still feel their claws scraping away at his skin and the leathery wings beating on his face as they raced around the small room. And it proved to be a fallacy that bats never got tangled in a person's hair.

He could still hear the supposedly soundless screeching and the panicked and vicious flapping in his left ear, as one hideous little creature got its leg caught in his hair, or his earpiece, or something else. It'd been more panicked than him probably, but that didn't take away from the fact these things were creepy, dirty vermin.

He swiveled left and right searching for the flying thing, his heart smashing against his chest. The flashlight's white light skimmed over the area where he thought it had landed.

There was nothing to see, except a weathered wooden fence with two broken slats and weeds clawing at its base. A fist-sized rock, below what looked like a fresh dent in the wood, caught his attention. He leaned forward to pick it up when a pain flared at the side of his neck. Another projectile of some sort hit him.

"Ahh! Shee-it. What the—?"

Not a bullet, entered his mind again. Hurt like shit though.

Then another struck him, this time on his thigh. He had begun to duck, but this one had unbalanced him, and as he stumbled to his left, he instinctively flung a palm toward the fence to stop his fall. It worked, and he managed to steady himself.

In the dark and confusion, his hand fell away from his gun but he didn't notice. A sigh of relief escaped his lips, a grateful sigh that he'd remained on his feet. Now, as he gathered his thoughts, he ran several steps forward, hugging the fence line before falling to a bent-knee stance.

One palm, fingers spread, held flat against the fence for support as he raised the flashlight in the other and aimed it up the alley in the direction from which the rocks had come. His outstretched hand wavered before his chest, creating dancing balls of light in the air.

And there he was...

The beam exposed a man in a red plaid shirt and torn-at-the-knee jeans. He stood, feet planted apart like a cowboy at a showdown.

Well, at least it was just one, or so it appeared. Not a "kid" kid, but still young, and Frank had been trained for this situation.

Plaid Shirt had used force, so Frank was entitled to protect his own life exactly as he saw fit. And he saw fit to draw his gun and wouldn't hesitate to use it, either.

He thought to hit the panic button on his portable radio, even slid his left hand to his shoulder and rested a finger there. Pressing this would alert dispatch and a 10-13 would hit the airwaves. Then every cop within several miles' vicinity would come racing to his assistance.

But he didn't want to do that because, hey, Frank could handle himself and talk this guy around. Plaid Shirt looked more frightened than threatening. Besides, sometimes events could become unpredictable when you got a bunch of squad cars converging and everybody ready to come to the aid of a fellow officer in danger. He didn't want this kid's life on his conscience if things went bad.

Yeah, he could do this, so he lowered his hand because a split-second was all Frank required to reach for his gun and release the lock on the holster. This a-hole would be so very sorry—

"Shit," he said beneath his breath.

He knew at that moment that he'd made a mistake. As he stumbled those few feet back after being hit, the gun must have fallen. He glanced back to the spot by the fence, but it was hard to see in this darkness.

Not for a single second did he move that flashlight from Plaid Shirt. He couldn't let him know he was unarmed. He hoped the light would distract the asshole and he wouldn't realize what Frank was doing in looking behind.

Oh, and there it was. In the dim back-glow, he spied it lying five, six feet away, too far for him to reach without turning around and taking his focus off his friend.

He had no choice though, he decided. This Mexican standoff wouldn't last forever. Somebody was going to make a move and if this guy had the guts to be flinging projectiles at a cop, then who knew what he might try next?

Frank bent his body to the right and began to rise in what felt like slow motion. Plaid Shirt must have anticipated this move; without warning, he charged. Frank had hoped that this one would be like most offenders and run when the opportunity for escape presented itself. So, what the hell was this guy thinking?

Frank didn't have time to reach his gun; he was about to be bowled over by the insane son of a bitch. The flashlight gripped in his hand was his only defense. So, he stood to full height, planted his feet and whipped the flashlight behind his body in a perfect arc, ready to swing.

Plaid Shirt was fast though, all pumped up on drugs, no doubt, PCP or some kind of synthetic shit. That stuff could turn a normal person into the Hulk. This whole casual, *I'll just clear the lane and go home* had gone bad real quick.

Frank stepped back, somehow managing to put his foot on uneven ground or another rock. He overbalanced. His arms flew up to counter and—coming from a deep, instinctive part of his brain—as an effort to fend off an attacker charging like a rhino.

His chest and right shoulder bore the impact of the hundred and forty pounds of body. It felt like a flying baby elephant had hit him as his legs crumpled beneath his body and he fell backward into the fence. The back of his head smashed into the hard ground, but a thick patch of weeds saved his skull from cracking open like a dropped egg.

Thank God for lazy gardeners.

He saw stars and moons and a kaleidoscope of color swirling in his vision. Pain fired, like a half-dozen sharp needles jammed into his neck. And *get up,* screamed inside his head.

Get up get up get up!

He tried. He really tried, with every ounce of energy, awareness, and life force in his body.

The flashlight was gone, fallen from his grasp and rolled well away, a few feet beyond his reach. It now lay in the opposite direction of his gun's position, the beam skimming across the uneven, laneway asphalt.

But his mind was back, and he had but a split-second decision to make: which way to roll?

His attacker had fallen too but was getting up, only three or four steps from the gun. Frank wondered if Plaid Shirt knew he'd been separated from his weapon, this being the reason for the man's aggressive move. If he did know, then Frank was in real trouble because he'd never get to it first.

Okay, forget that, he thought, as he raised himself onto his knees and crawled, dog-fashion toward his flashlight. In a pinch, it could double as a baton.

God, I'm a fool. This story was never being shared with Lucy. She wouldn't let him out the door ever again. He'd have to come up with some reason for the bruises he knew would appear after this tussle.

Only a couple more feet and he'd be there. He lunged forward, fell to his stomach and, with outstretched fingers, reached out...

...just a few more inches. Just a few.

C'mon, do it!

He felt the touch of the cold metal on his fingertips and...

Bang...

Something hard and rough hit him in the side of the head, just above his temple.

Flashes of light exploded behind his eyes again and deep in his brain, blurring his vision. Crisp, white shards of pain ricocheted inside his skull. The sun and Lucy's face were all he saw. He thought how happy she looked that he'd agreed to the beach vacation.

The throbbing ache pulled him back into the lane. Thin rivulets of warmth slid down his forehead and cheeks . He smelled the crisp metallic scent of what seemed to be a lot of blood on his face. He no doubt suffered a concussion, but he could still see and his senses were intact.

He grunted as he folded one knee beneath his body to rise. Two seconds, three, were all he needed to gather his wits. The attacker had retreated, so he had time.

Retreating because he realizes I'm a cop, I bet.

Then another thought exploded, a terrible realization that maybe Plaid Shirt had...

The gun!

He needed to get to it before the asshole. Frank wouldn't shoot him if he could help it. No, he'd just make sure he knew never to attack anyone who wore blue again.

In his peripheral vision, he caught a glimpse of his foe. Ten feet off to his right, he stood still staring Frank's way. Why hadn't he cockroach-scuttled away? Frank debated whether that was good or bad as he rose to a crouch, fingers spread with tips resting on the ground to steady himself.

No, it had to be bad. The guy must know he was police, yet didn't seem to care.

Frank was in a seriously deep water. He understood this as a needle phobic understands a dentist's reassurance of *a little sting,* just before it burns like he's shoved a shard of hot metal into the gum. This was *a shitload of trouble* for Frank because he had nothing left with which to fight. His legs had turned to jelly, filled with rubber bones. If he couldn't stand, this would go from scary to terrifying in three breaths.

This had gone way past playing around. His hand fought him as he slipped it up to his shoulder and fumbled with the radio.

Yes! There was the panic button. He depressed it and breathed out a sigh, relieved to know help would be here in minutes. They had his position, and the moment this shithead heard the sirens, he'd scuttle away like all good cockroaches.

All Frank needed to do was keep his wits about him until backup reached him. Hopefully, by the time the others arrived, he would have managed to get this guy down and in cuffs. Nothing worse than looking as though some idiot got the better of you. And he probably shouldn't have come down this lane on his own either, so he'd prefer not to explain that in a report.

He looked up and around, his gaze drawn to the last place he'd seen the gun. Yes, it was still there, now only two yards or so from him but unfortunately also between him and Plaid Shirt. So, he too could reach the weapon if he saw it.

There was no choice. Frank lunged, throwing his full weight into the momentum and praying adrenaline would harden his limbs. Both hands scraped the ground as he slid out of control. His palms burned, and he knew the rough surface was peeling away layers of skin.

But he almost had the gun. Sweet Jesus, he would have his weapon. His fingers touched the cold metal and the digits scrambled with a mind of their own to find a hold.

He almost had a grasp on the damned thing when the boot stomped down on his knuckles. He heard a crack and the pain was immediate and shocking, causing him to let go.

The same boot disappeared back into the darkness as Frank squealed in pain and grabbed for his broken hand. Only a second or two passed before the boot returned, this time swinging across in front of his face.

He covered his head with both hands for protection but wasn't struck. Then he saw why. The boot had swung sideways this time, at the gun. Plaid Shirt had a great aim too because the weapon hurtled off into the darkness, well away from Frank's reach.

But he wasn't giving up without a fight, injuries aside, because here was his chance.

With surprising speed, he climbed to his feet, careful not to put his injured hand on the ground as support. The man's back was to him as he went after Frank's gun again. So, Frank threw himself at the attacker just as he bent to retrieve the weapon.

"Fuck yooo," he screamed, as their bodies connected, and he sent the asshole sprawling into the opposite fence which, as fortune would have it, was a brick wall. Several bricks toppled from the top, one hitting his attacker's arm and another his shoulder. Though he remained standing, it was distraction enough that the man paused for a split-second. This then allowed Frank the time to squat and scoop up his gun.

Now he'd be okay. Now he could take control of the situation and get this maniac into custody. This time, he held his weapon tight as he ducked to his right out of range of the guy's hands which were already outstretched and reaching for him.

"Not today, asshole," Frank said with a growl so like Clint Eastwood or a *Die Hard* Bruce Willis that he almost smiled. And if it wasn't for the darkness, he would have been fine. In the half-light though, and with the blow to his head, his coordination was off; his foot connected with something hard and sharp, a brick fallen from the wall.

"Oh, shit," he said as he felt himself falling and reached down with his good hand, trying to protect the broken one.

He fell well, if there was such a thing, and hit the asphalt and rolled.

Still got the gun. Still okay.

Now lying on his side, he was uncertain of Plaid Shirt's position and so, again, he was in great peril. Not wanting to let go of his pistol, he pushed into the gritty road surface with his bad hand and grunted from the agony that shot up his arm.

Jesus, Mother of God, he would kill this asshole if he ever got his hands on him.

In the distance, he thought he heard the faintest wail of a siren, so faint he wasn't sure if he even imagined it. Good, though; if he was right, the asshole would hear as well and take off now. *Run away, why don't you,* he was about to scream, because he just wanted to get home to Lucy now. He didn't want to fight with some loser over a damaged building which could be easily repaired.

The displacement of moving air nearby alerted him just before the foot connected with his shoulder, the one with the good hand holding the gun. The blow sent him tumbling backward. Adrenaline pumped into his system like a keyed-on injection engine, and it momentarily surprised him how little pain he felt considering his mounting injuries.

Broken bones and gravel rash were the least of his worries though; *damn it to hell*, he'd lost his weapon. *Yeah, again.*

What he needed to know right now was if Plaid Shirt had gotten a hold of it. But he didn't know where the guy was because it was so dark, and he felt shell-shocked and confused. And his eyes had what he presumed was blood from a severe head wound seeping into them, clouding his vision.

This had officially become any cop's worst nightmare.

VACATION

2012 PART 3

Frank had mere moments to take control of the situation.

This wasn't a normal assailant. If he couldn't retrieve the gun or get out of this lane, he understood on a subliminal level that his life was in real danger. You trained for a circumstance such as this, but you never believed it could or would happen—not in an alley, thirty minutes before the end of your shift.

Nope, you don't imagine this scenario.

Keep a cool head, they tell you. Don't panic. Panic can kill you.

Yeah, no kidding, kemosabe!

All good and well when you're practicing with a buddy under fluorescent lighting in an air-conditioned gym. But in the dark with a drugged-out irrational lunatic, well, that was just asking a hell of a lot of the average guy. Ten seconds remained between him and screaming, and even then, that was optimistic.

He groped frantically around in search of the gun or a rock or any darn thing he could use to defend himself. Plaid Shirt was nearby, he knew that, sensed it with every nerve of his body. He felt the imaginary breath on the nape of his neck. A breeze was more likely, but he still reached blindly behind to clutch for an ankle and topple his adversary. If he brought him to the ground, both then on the same level, he stood a chance. There was nothing there though.

Things can't get any worse than this, he thought, as he wiped away blood gathered on his brow.

And then they did get worse.

The terrified scream of a female startled him.

His head arched from the ground and swiveled in the scream's direction. A gate was open two property lines along and across from where he lay. There, in the illumination of the flashlight, stood a woman in jogging pants and a sweater, her fist stuffed into her mouth. Even through his clouded, bloodied vision, he saw her eyes were wild and wide with fear.

Frank's nature to care more about others than himself was a powerful force, and so his first thought was to ensure a bystander's safety above even his own survival.

"Get back. Not safe," he managed to shout, as he maneuvered a hand beneath himself. Before he'd pushed up, a boot came from the side behind him and stomped down, crushing his damaged fingers again.

He groaned as sharp, bitter agony shot up his arm. But his cry was cut short by the impact of a body landing on top of him.

Jesus, is this guy insane?

Punches rained down on him as he pushed at and tussled with the man. Frank retaliated with elbows, knees, anything he could use to free himself and dislodge the attacker. For a moment, he caught a glance of the woman still standing there, hesitating. Why didn't she turn away and get to safety? Call for help? She was in shock, quite possibly.

Then she was gone from sight, his view blocked by his insane foe. This close up, he saw that although the man was big, he was also young. Late teens, early twenties, dark hair. And he had been right about the drugs. The assailant's dilated pupils, along with the sweat beading his face, and skin that looked as though it hadn't seen the sun in a month, were sure signs.

Frank knew he needed to free his arms in order to land a solid punch, so he could get up and find his gun. In a miracle, as if his thought had commanded circumstance, he untangled a hand from the tussle. He swung once and connected with his opponent's ribs, hearing a low grunt as Plaid Shirt's grip loosened.

He pulled his arm back again, in his rush scraping his knuckles along the rough gravel surface. Adrenaline dampened the hurt, but he'd hesitated and was too slow. That was age for you. Three sharp punches to his chin, cheek and chest smacked Frank into the ground.

Multi-colored sparklers lit up his vision. He wondered if somebody had fired a flare because everything, fences, the sky, even Plaid Shirt's face, glowed red and orange.

This guy hit like a pro-boxer, but this old cowboy wasn't going down without a fight. When his attacker swung again, Frank blocked with his elbow and kicked out with a leg. Instinct more than training commanded his moves.

It worked. The weight rolled from his chest, followed by retreating footsteps. Relief filled the moment as his breath came rapid and heavy as he fought for calm. His head was clearing a little, and he pulled himself up more like an arthritic eighty-year-old than a trained law enforcement officer.

One knee first, then a hand pushing firmly into the ground. His balance wavered, and he paused in that position to gather himself and find his breath, still coming ragged and short.

Shit, I'm getting too old to fight like this.

Yeah, like he got into this type of fight every day. *Not.*

Video surveillance would pick Plaid Shirt up later somewhere. He'd got a good look at his face too. He was big, and in a line-up, he'd be not too difficult to recognize.

Frank shifted his weight and managed to pull himself to his feet. The throb in his jaw suggested he'd broken it too. He needed to get to the car and call for backup. He could use his personal radio here but that would distract him and leave him vulnerable.

"Oh, my God!"

Jeez, he'd forgotten the woman. He heard her voice before he saw her. She still stood at the gate but resembled a ghost. He wondered if the knocks to his head had created a mirage.

His first emotion was annoyance that she hadn't listened to him. He thought to shout, *when a police officer tells you to move, you move!* But he realized she wasn't looking at him; she stared past him, in the direction the flashlight still shone.

A niggling buzz inside his brain screamed that something was wrong. He turned his head to follow her gaze. Even with his body only half-rotated, he saw over his shoulder what had frightened her so much.

Plaid Shirt stood a few yards beyond her in the middle of the lane. In his hand, he held Frank's gun; on his face, he wore a look of profound amusement. The barrel, aimed directly at Frank, shook in the grasp of someone who was away with the meth-fairies.

Now he was sure he heard sirens. They were still some distance away but coming. Yes, they were coming. Maybe a minute or so out. Plaid Shirt must hear them too, and now he would leave, surely.

Just run away, like every other idiot criminal, will ya!

Frank turned slowly to face him square-on. Then he began to back up toward the woman. Something in Plaid Shirt's stance said he wanted far more than a one-minute struggle on the ground in a neighborhood alley.

A few more steps back, then a couple more to his right would bring Frank close to the civilian. Then he would just need to throw himself at her and hopefully land them both inside her yard.

Why she stayed standing there beyond belief, but he didn't dare speak to her and divert his focus from a man who had Frank's own weapon in his grasp. Frank held out half-raised hands, palms facing out in surrender, to show he was unarmed and also send a message for the guy to *calm the hell down*.

In a voice calmer than he felt, he said, "That's not a good idea, son. You know how many cops'll come after you if you make a wrong decision here? Give me the gun... and lets you and me talk. I'll just call this a misunderstanding and we'll walk away. I startled you. Not your fault. I can see that. Can't you? Perhaps you can argue self-defense. I won't deny that. We'll work that out. Okay? Put the gun down on the ground. You turn around and go."

The sound of the weapon discharging echoed in the still night, shocking and surreal. There was a punch in his chest like a big bird had banged into him. What sprung to mind was the image of a crow that had once smashed into a house window his wife had just cleaned. Broke its poor neck.

There was no pain, so he figured it was another big rock hurled at him. How Plaid Shirt had done that while holding a gun was pretty impressive.

Frank had never been shot before. Not even stabbed. Nothing. The worst injuries before this were a smashed-up jaw and those broken fingers from only a few minutes ago.

His first thought was, *thank God he missed.*

His second, *all negotiation off the table.*

He made a dive to the left, intent on hurling himself toward the woman's gate. This would kill two birds with one stone, not a great metaphor for this exact moment but he wasn't in total control of his faculties and needed to get them both to safety. The situation had gotten real crazy, real quick.

But his balance seemed very off and he couldn't seem to move his legs the way he wanted, the way he needed, to propel himself toward her.

The *thwack* of the two impacts startled him before he realized that sound was the gun firing again. One caught him in the leg, another in the shoulder. Not critical injury shots but enough to throw him backward and cause him to overbalance. This time, he fell with no control like a discarded rag doll. Unable to break his fall, his head slammed hard onto the harsh, unforgiving surface.

He lay there, sucking air in and out. In and out.

To his immediate right was where he'd last seen the woman. She had also fallen to the ground and now faced him. He wanted to assure her and tell her they'd be fine, that help was on its way. But he saw that wouldn't be necessary.

For a confused second, Frank imagined he looked into his own wife's eyes. *Lovely Lucy*, as he often thought of her, reached a languid arm toward him on the beach. The warmth of the sand, combined with the sun beating down on his back, recalled to his mind the smell of ham cooking on a grill. And the surprising cold of the ocean lapping at his toes felt so darn good.

"Time for cocktails, darling?" she said.

"No, it's a beer for me, Woman. You know that."

He tried to call out to the nearby waiter, but a chill had traveled up his legs, and he didn't want to move just yet.

Come back, sun, he thought as a shiver overcame him; it was not so comfortable in the water anymore.

"Time for cocktails," she said again.

Now those words annoyed him. He'd just told her he wanted a beer. He shook his head, closed his eyes and willed his patience to take control. They were on vacation and he wasn't behaving like the man of her dreams.

Back in the direction of the hotel, he heard a wha-wha, wha-wha sound. It reminded him of a siren. Were they having a fire drill? What kind of resort was this that they ran drills in the middle of the day? Who was gonna be in their room at this time? And it was growing louder. Far out, he could barely hear himself think.

He looked at his legs, now frozen to the bone, and decided to return to the hotel foyer and complain about the noise, inform them that there should be some warning to guests.

When he gazed over to his wife to tell her so, he realized he lay beside a stranger.

This wasn't a beach and the woman staring at him was saying nothing to anyone ever again.

A stray bullet? Damn, this is a true tragedy...

"Time to say bye-bye," Lucy said, and there was his girl again. She shook her head like he'd done something wrong, but drinking a beer instead of a fancy combination of spirits with a cutesy umbrella was no reason for her to be annoyed.

Not drinking a cocktail was no big deal. What the hell does she expect?

No, no, he had this wrong. That wasn't his wife's voice. The condescending tone was Plaid Shirt's. And that was a big deal because he hadn't run away.

Damn him, why hasn't he run?

Frank tried to get up, wanting to shove his fist into the drugged-out idiot's face and hang being an honest cop. He'd shoot the asshole in the head if he could get hold of his gun again.

"Time to say bye-bye," the man repeated, his voice now overhead.

"You go, go... fye-fye, firsss, you an-im-al," Frank growled, but it came out as a sputter of half-formed words. Thick mucus glued his mouth together like he'd swallowed a jar of peanut butter. Blood, he guessed.

The cold had traveled up through his arms and he wished he had a blanket. No pain though, which surprised him. Frank didn't want to die here alone in an alley for no good reason, while Lucy waited, worrying about just such a thing happening.

If he couldn't get home to her, she'd always wonder if his last moments were agony. He wished he could leave a note.

It's fine, love. Really. No suffering.

So nearby, he could almost feel the vibrations, the sirens announced his rescuers' approach, but they were too late. He understood that so clearly because if Plaid Shirt was going to leave, he would have gone by now.

Frank reached toward the woman, pulling himself with his uninjured arm but he made little headway, which seemed pretty funny to him as he thought that. *Should be called arm-way.*

He began to laugh but a crack like a breaking branch stopped him.

He thought to warn Lucy. "Here comes a coconut. Better duck."

The shot didn't register in his mind because he'd returned to the beach.

Ah, warm sand.

Cool water was slipping up and over his body, then drawing back to trickle away beneath his legs, and around his feet and through his toes. This time, the temperature was perfect. He might just have that cocktail to keep Lovely Lucy happy. She deserved happiness.

He pondered returning to the hotel to take a grandpa nap before dinner. She wouldn't mind. Maybe he'd get a jacket because his chest had begun to feel shiver-cold.

Nah, let's stay here a little longer.

The sun was warm. He was glad he'd given in to his wife and they'd chosen the beach vacation. This break was well-earned. He'd given too much of himself to his job and not enough to Lucy. And this was a good feeling, to lay down his head without a care in the world.

He made himself a promise, there and then, on that beach in the sun, lying by the only woman he'd ever loved, *would* ever love. *Not so long between vacations, Frank Chester,* he told himself. *Life's too damned short.*

DEMON

"You gotta be shitting me!" Michael hissed.

To which Pezzullo replied, "This one's the next available auto-mo-beel. What is-a the pro-blem-o?"

He pronounced every word as if he was talking to a three-year-old. The guy wasn't even police, but nothing more than a garage attendant for the service vehicles.

He'd spoken with him many times when checking out a car from the central garage and he always seemed to use a mocking tone, like he was the superior. Michael had taken to pretending he was on his phone or in a hurry, so their interaction was minimal.

The first time they'd met was his second day after completing training. Back then, his excitement caused him to ignore the sneer and the up-and-down look given him as if the dick had smelled something rotten. Pezzullo had gripped Michael's shoulder and told him to take proper care of the City's property or he'd dent his skull. The big-nosed idiot laughed as he spoke, but he was beefy and solid, and a little intimidating. Michael imagined he'd enjoy making good on his promise.

In the past six weeks, with his enthusiasm all but drained to empty, he was just pissed that yet again his luck had soured as he was handed the keys to 291.

"I think you know the problem."

Pezzullo stared like a dumb ape.

"With 291?" Michael said. "Heap of junk. The shitty thing hates me."

"Don't imagine a car can hate you. *I* could hate you for your crummy jokes. Whining doesn't endear ya much, either, if we're discussing pet peeves. Absolutely nuttin' wrong with this. Something' wrong with you, maybe."

That stung. Michael had shared a few words of wit, trying to assimilate into what seemed like a club with unspoken rules. He was new and sensed his co-workers judging him. The camaraderie he'd imagined from watching all the cop shows and listening to his dad was cool to non-existent now. In fact, it seemed to grow even more distant as time went by.

In the first few weeks, it seemed okay, but ever since 291 entered his life on a regular basis, things seemed to have changed. The wind changed, or a solar flare happened, or somebody got their nose out of joint. Suddenly, he was on the outside looking in.

Well, he didn't give two fucks then, because he didn't think he'd done or said anything to offend anyone. *Who knew though, right?* They could just all be assholes and didn't get his sense of humor.

Sometimes, when he passed by a few of the guys at headquarters or the canteen, he thought he overheard them whispering about him. He imagined his name along with a few sniggers hanging in the air like a thick, stinking fart. Occasionally, he'd check his back in the bathroom mirror, in case someone had been childish enough to stick one of those stupid, *kick me* signs on his back. He wouldn't put it past them. But there was never anything there.

Too sensitive, Mike, he assured himself. *You're just the new guy.*

Maybe there was something, but he just couldn't put his finger on it. He blamed 291 for setting him on edge and screwing with his mind.

As he stared back at Pezzullo, trying to hide how annoyed the guy made him, he almost asked him what his problem was, but then he knew the answer. Ass-hole-itis. The jerk continued with his speech as if he was giving a Ted Talk, and Michael wished he'd kept his mouth shut about the fucking car.

"...I think the Captain could easily hate you for being such a whining little baby. But I don't beh-leeve a *ve-hi-cle* can hate you. Fugget-about-it! This isn't *Christine*, spooky cruiser comes to life and tries to kill you."

Michael shook his head and offered a smile. He gave a chuckle, even, when he'd prefer to punch the King Asshole right in his fat, pockmarked nose.

"Listen, I've had 291 at least eight times in the past couple of weeks. Don't know why I'm so unlucky, but every one of those times, this car has broken down or caused me hell."

"What's the matter, with you? You got some voodoo hex on you."

He held his hands up and waggled his fingers like a magician about to reveal a hidden object.

"Sleep with the wrong girl, did ya? Speak ill of the dead, huh? Because, friend, you're the only one with these issues. Kinda disrespectful too, this being a meem-oar-eeal ve-hi-cle. *You know what I mean!*"

He said "you know what I mean" as a statement not a question. Again, he was off with the speaking as if Michael was a hick. Why couldn't he just say vehicle like it was just a word and not a threat? Just plain *vehicle.*

Of course, he knew it was a memorial car. No doubt, that was why this hunk of junk remained in service well past its use-by date. Yeah, yeah, he should show more reverence for the symbolism, he guessed. Sure, he had respect and sympathy for the poor guy who'd died. Said respect though, did not extend to the motherfucking car the guy was driving when he met his end.

"I meant no disrespect to the man's memory. I'm honored to drive his patrol vehicle but..."

"You had better be honored. Frank Chester was the best cop you're likely to meet. *Period.* Ran rings around ninety percent of 'em. I'll tell you, the man would not be whining his ride *hated* him. Let's hope you never discover what matters when one of your buddies loses his life for nothing. *Nu-thing*." Pezzullo emphasized his speech with hands slicing the air, adding inarguable punctuating to his speech.

Michael stared at the guy's chin, feeling two inches shorter. He avoided further eye contact as he swiped the keys from Pezzullo's outstretched hand with a little more force than he intended.

"Hey, if you're thinking you wanna break up with your ve-hi-cle... go right ahead. Put your complaint in writing to the Sergeant. See what he says. If you want my humble opinion though... Fugget-about-it!"

Michael stood there longer than felt comfortable while he tried to come up with something to smooth over this interaction. He didn't need Pezzullo talking about him to the other cops. His imagination saw the idiot speaking like a ten-year-old girl as he exaggerated this exchange.

Gossip was no doubt all the genius had in his life. What did he do for ten hours a day, anyway? Sat around on his fat ass handing out keys and wishing he was a real cop.

But the guy had upset him, and nothing sprang to his flustered mind. That was except, *fuck you for your help with the demon ve-hi-cle.*

So, *thanks* was all he replied as a particularly weak comeback; although sarcasm dripped from that single word.

He turned and walked away toward the lot, keys gripped in his sweating palm, and imagined Pezzullo spitting after him as he whispered *fuck for brains* under his breath.

291 awaited him in bay fourteen. Just looking at the grille and headlights made him imagine something was alive inside the metal molecules, waiting for him. *Come in, come in, and play with me, my little toy cop.* He could almost visualize malice coursing through the fuel pump and wiring, a wild stallion stamping its legs in anticipation of the trainer who would try but fail to break him. It was a rabid dog, frothing, backing up, ready to pounce. A bull, head down, hoof sliding across the arena's crushed-rock surface as it faced the matador.

He stopped and shook his head. What was he really thinking? His mind was playing tricks on him because the car wasn't that at all. This was nothing more than a sorry excuse for a *ve-hi-cle,* with seven-year-old scratches, deep scuff marks and only ten miles short of two hundred thousand on the clock.

He angled his neck to the side and stared at the smiling portrait on the rear, right panel. His fingers trailed over the stickered words.

In Memoriam
Frank Chester 1971–2012
Never forgotten.

His murder formed part of recruits' training. In their first week out of the academy, every rookie went out onto the streets with Frank's image and name in the forefront of their mind. *Why his death happened and how to avoid it happening to you. Whether the officer should have entered the alley without backup? The precautions to take so a perp couldn't access your weapon. How the civilian death might have been prevented in that case and in the future.*

It all sounded to Michael like a simple case of dumb luck. It was just like him to get a poor sap's car more than his fair share of the time. The bad fortune of poor old Frank Chester had somehow passed over to him. Why he deserved this, he hadn't a clue. Could it be his ever-increasing bad attitude to the job? Then again, it was mostly the car's fault he hated coming to work these days, so it was a big Catch-22.

Or Catch-291.

He smiled at his own wit.

The question he'd begun to ask himself was whether this constant issue with the car proved he'd chosen the wrong career?

His mind wandered to the idea that if he ignored the hints, he might end up as another Officer Chester. Instead of the bravery award he'd dreamed of receiving as a kid, they'd use his name to teach *what not to do.* Dumbass award coming his way!

As he climbed into the cab and started the engine, a thought flashed into his head. *This was no coincidence.* Hadn't that guest speaker during his third week at the Academy said that?

"There are no coincidences." The detective had repeated it twenty times in the ninety minutes he was on stage.

What was his name? O, something...

O'Grady. Detective Lance O'Grady. The now decorated cop who a few years back had solved those weird mass killings all occurring in the same city in the same month. Now that would have made interesting work. He should call O'Grady to solve the case of the haunted 291.

Yes, he had begun to figure he should heed the signs. He should listen to 291 and Frank Chester's ghost, or demon, or whatever lived in this fucking stupid car.

If you don't face facts, you'll end up dead in an alley somewhere, bullet-ridden and ruing your mistakes. That was what he'd started telling himself.

Could be it wasn't just a message for him but a full-on possession with a spirit who wrought disaster on anyone getting into the car, this being the real reason behind Chester's death, that the devil's disciple hated cops. He wished he could speak to the poor schmuck and swap notes. Had he ignored the same warnings now being sent to Michael?

As he reversed from the parking spot, he was so engrossed in his thoughts that he swung the wheel harder and with less care than normal. A harsh, metallic, scraping squeal came from the right fender as it kissed the concrete pylon.

"Take that," he said under his breath, not giving a shit. "Give it your best shot. I'm no whiny little baby."

This car had picked the wrong cop because he wasn't about to let this persecution continue. In the next few days, he'd come up with something, even if it killed him. And he had no intention of getting himself killed anytime soon.

LUNCH

Eric Pickett had been the one to cement the idea in Michael's head. That he was in serious trouble had been floating around inside his mind all today, after 291 had yet again been assigned to him. After his unpleasant interaction with Pezzullo the Asshole, he had to come up with a solution because his head was filling with constant images of his own death. Each event was more gruesome than the previous.

This was the fourth time he and his new friend had grabbed a bite to eat. They patrolled in the same area, and since he enjoyed Italian as much as Michael, it made sense. He wasn't as aloof as the other guys at his precinct. In fact, Eric had sought Michael out and invited him for a drink a few weeks ago.

La Roma was not what you'd call a great restaurant; maybe it came close to *good*, but not quite. They served quick food without fuss and the pizza wasn't half bad, and that was enough when you were on a break. Oh, and Eric apparently had hopes with a busty, blond waitress of sharing a more intimate interaction than *can I take your order*. The description could apply to her too. Not great, not quite good. But with those wide hips, comfortable and good enough—if you were in a hurry.

Today, Michael had finally shared the story of his *haunted* cruiser with Pickett, although he'd left out the scraping of the front panel in the garage earlier that day.

Eric listened without interruption or laughter like a real friend. Michael had begun to trust him and felt here was someone he could respect. Maybe only a few years younger than him, thirty-two, thirty-three, he'd already been on the force for a decade.

He had that way of looking at you that said, *I've seen so much, I'm not into bullshit.* But he wasn't at his father's jaded, don't-ask-any-more-questions stage yet. He still seemed to enjoy sharing interesting tales from his career. This gave Michael the permission to not need to pretend everything was hunky-fucking-dory.

Eric had been the one who'd brought up the car on their first meeting, which was weeks ago now. It was at the Starbucks counter on West Nineteenth Street while waiting for his order. Someone had slapped him too hard on his back and said, "How ya doin', friend?"

He'd spun around, hand moving at once to his belt, ready to pull out his baton, when he realized the voice belonged to another cop.

Michael clutched at his chest in an exaggerated manner, smiled and said, "Oh man, you scared me."

The stranger smirked.

"Sorry. I've seen you 'round, but I haven't introduced myself. You were in the last graduating group, right? I'm Eric Pickett."

"Michael Chambers. Mike. Yeah. Finding my feet."

He'd shaken the extended hand from the fellow officer with the toothy grin and what could only be described as a mischievous twinkle in his eyes.

"Saw 291 outside. A sad history with Chester."

That first time Eric had mentioned Frank Chester, Michael had paid little attention. It was a casual reference, nothing more, this meeting having happened before things began to suspiciously go wrong. They exchanged pleasantries and swapped cell numbers right there in the coffee line.

When things did start to happen, he'd hesitated to confide 291's misdemeanors because his new friend was always so upbeat. While his fellow officers seemed distant, Eric's enthusiasm and friendliness were welcome, and he didn't want to jeopardize their new relationship.

But yesterday, after 291 delivered another flat tire—the third in three weeks—he couldn't help himself. He had to say something to somebody because dealing with this on his own was becoming too much. These past few nights, he hadn't slept well, and his pants were looser even though he was sure he was eating the same as usual.

The stress must have reached the point where it showed because the minute they'd sat down, his friend had asked the inevitable. "Everything okay, buddy? Don't answer that. You look like shit. Been on a bender?"

"You could say that," he'd replied, pondering if he should be honest.

Bender. Yes, that was the exact effect this constant battle with the car had on him. He felt as if he'd been bent around a pole, this way and that. After all the wrenching, his emotions were knotted up like a mangled, twisted straw.

Michael rubbed a hand across his forehead.

Should I tell him?

He pushed the question around while Eric's gaze locked on him. There was that twinkle in his eye again like the entire world was amusing; his attitude was almost innocent as if there was nothing that didn't have a solution.

"Something happen out there? Or is it a girl? Come on. Spill."

Okay, here goes.

He hoped he didn't regret the trust he was about to place in this man. With one deep breath, he held and then exhaled, letting his worries escape.

"No nothing to do with the job. Well, kinda, but not *the job*. You'll call me crazy."

He paused, rubbing at his lips before continuing. "Fuck, I *am* crazy... it's the car."

Pickett's head reared backward as if he'd been slapped. He furrowed his brow and asked, "What car?"

"Two. Nine. One."

Michael spat the numbers out as if sharing the name of a cheating girlfriend.

"Your... wait a minute. Squad vehicle? 291? I don't understand. What's going on?"

"I don't understand either, but I can't shake the feeling something is out to get me."

Oh, that sounded weird.

"Things just keep going wrong. Hard to believe, I know, but an automobile cannot break down, have multiple flat tires and stop dead for no reason as much as this one does. When the mechanic checks, the bitch is fine, y'know? Just as if it's always there, waiting to get one over on me."

"Okay, okay, so you're saying that, what, it's sabotaging you? A car?"

He laughed and patted the table several times. Michael wished he'd kept his mouth shut. Now it was out there, he doubted a single person would take him seriously. Heck, he didn't take *himself* seriously. It sounded even crazier spoken aloud. He'd really shared this because he wanted to know if there was a logical reason that hadn't occurred to him. Other than the haunted, Christine, fucking Stephen King similarity, which seemed about the only answer.

Well, it was out there, so he may as well finish it, he thought, so he added, "I feel as if I'm being watched. Is it a cop thing? Something I don't get because I'm a rookie? Stress response or some shit like that."

Eric's face softened, and the smirk disappeared, as he waved a hand between them as if swatting a fly away.

"Nah. Nah. Nah," Eric said, ending with an emphatic "No."

He leaned forward as if they were co-conspirators. "291, right? That's what you're saying?"

Michael nodded.

"Frank Chester's cruiser, yeah?"

He shook his head as he mentioned the murdered man. Of all things eliciting a melancholy response from a cop, saying a fallen colleague's name was top of the list.

"Yes. The one and only."

Eric seemed to ponder Michael's admission for a moment, even picking up his glass of coke and taking a swig before replying.

"You know, this may not be so crazy. I think I heard something on this."

It was Michael's turn to nod, to urge him to continue.

"A year ago, thereabouts, I didn't pay much attention. I haven't driven that car much, or if I have, I don't remember."

Eric made the sign of the cross over his chest and a burning coil tightened in Michael's stomach.

"Another guy had the same problem. Claimed he had a haunted vehicle. Now, who was that? Jatorio, or his partner? No, wait, Henderson. Yeah, yeah, yeah—Henderson."

He appeared proud for remembering. Then—suddenly—he stopped and tilted his head, gazing at the ceiling lost in thought. A few moments later, he returned to stare straight in Michael's eyes.

"I'm wrong. Not him, because he got moved over to Fourteenth Street. So, Johnson? No, no, that's not the one. Jokelini? Yeah, might be him. That sure rings a bell."

Pickett tapped the side of his forehead as if trying to knock the name loose.

"Nope, mind's a blank. Sorry. Anyway, whoever it was, something happened to him with that car. Don't know the exact details but it was freaky. For the life of me, I can't recall what the guy said, but I just remember thinking better him than me."

"Can you ask around who it might be? I'd like to meet him. Compare notes."

"Nah, if he was still here, I'd remember him. There's been no 291 talk in a long while. Except for that weird stuff that went down with the guy whose name I can't find in this dumb head of mine."

He gave a final shrug and said, "For now, that's all I got, buddy." Then he pushed a forkful of spaghetti into his mouth, chewed for a few seconds and stopped before pointing his fork at Michael.

With a full mouth of pasta, he added, "I'll ask around, but I tell you, I'm worried for you. What're you going to do? You can't let this thing get the better of you."

"What do you suggest?

"You really think it's haunted, huh?"

He shoved another mouthful of pasta between his lips and chewed with gusto.

Michael sighed, the wound-up coil inside released. For the first time in weeks, he felt as if he could breathe again. Finally, he'd shared, and somebody had listened. His confidence grew that he wasn't bordering on schizophrenia or some other mental illness. And a strange but compelling idea swirled in his mind and began to take shape.

"I'm not crazy," Michael said, his confidence in that sentence growing now that he'd said it to someone else. "And I need to do something."

Eric was still chewing as if his life depended on the food when he replied, so his first words were muffled. "Damn right. We don' wan' you becoming... 'notha... Frank Chester."

Then he swallowed and, now with gusto, added, "I mean, fuck the Department when they hand out a demon car to a rookie."

A glimmer of a mocking smile flickered at the corner of Eric's lips but then faded. Michael thought it was a natural response to personifying a lifeless, mechanical thing. And he knew that feeling well. Oh, but it was so great to have someone on his side.

Hope lifted in Michael, and it was in the nick of time. He'd run out of reasonable explanations, not that a haunted car was reasonable, but it was something that wasn't related to his mental state and that was encouraging. So that decided it. No more monkey-fucking with the heap of metal.

"You know," said his friend, waggling his finger between them. "Here's a thought. What if it's Frank Chester and he's not thrilled with strangers driving his car? Let's say he was a mean son-of-a-bitch and a dirty cop. Maybe the real truth is that it was a drug payoff gone wrong in that alley. They never caught the shooter, so—"

"You think? That's a good theory."

"Unsure, but I'll help you. I'm intrigued now. Let me dig around and ask a few guys. Wear my detective badge."

"Something else too—" offered Michael, so relieved he had found a confidant. He even glimpsed a future where the two of them worked together as detectives like on *Law and Order*. Not the original but *Criminal Intent*—major crimes, the big, exciting cases.

"Get it off your chest," said Eric in an encouraging tone.

"There's a presence. Weird sensation of breathing on the back of my neck. I'm sure once I even heard something whisper right in my ear. One night I was sitting in the car by Bayswater Park, near where they had those ongoing letterbox robberies? Freaked the hell out of me."

"Know the place... and wow!"

"I felt this scraping on my arm. A huge motherfuckin' spider was my first thought. You should have seen me move. Hurricane Michael was leaping out of that car as if it was on fire. Shone my flashlight in and checked everywhere."

"And?"

"Nothing. If it was there, I'd have seen it because it felt huge."

"That is freaky."

"After talking to you and with everything you've said, I don't believe I had an encounter with a creepy-crawly of the earthly kind. There was an entity in that car with me and it didn't have eight legs."

"That's insane, man. In all my time, I never experienced that. Something's wrong with the car then, buddy."

Encouraged by Eric's rapt attention, Michael spoke with certainty. "You know the novel that King guy wrote about a Plymouth Fury?"

He saw Pezzullo's face, the lame-brain garage attendant, as Michael was forced to admit he'd never heard of the book. He'd looked it up on Google and read the synopsis on the Wikipedia page. *What an imagination that King guy had*, he'd thought.

"King, yeah, I know him," said Eric, nodding with enthusiasm. "They made that creepy movie, *It* from one of his, right? Can't say I've heard of the book. Fun read?"

"If freaking you out is a version of good, then yes. Until today, I've told no-one about it."

"I'm sorry for you, man, and especially being a rookie. What're you going to do? Don't complain to the boss, that's my suggestion. They'll think you got a screw loose, and you'll get a psych eval. Every time you're up for promotion, it'll be there, stinkin' things up like shit on a shoe. Y'know how it goes; you think you got rid of it, then you round a corner and there's that shit stink again, followin' you. But I'm on your side and I'll ask around. Perhaps you just need to be patient and this'll blow over. Frank Chester's ghost might find someone else to bother."

"Or the demon will return to hell." Michael laughed. "Hey, just talking has helped."

"Yeah, anytime. I guess you can hope the car is in an accident and ends up a write-off."

"Wouldn't that be my lucky day?"

"In the meantime," said Eric, as he rose from his chair having demolished his entire bowl during their discussion, while Michael had barely touched his. "I gotta piss."

As he walked toward the bathroom, he stopped a few tables away and stretched out his arms, dangling his hands ninety-degrees from his wrists. Then he shuffled forward on stiffened legs.

He looked over his shoulder and said, "Hope the boogeyman don't get you before I come back. Your turn to pay."

Michael barely registered his words because a new idea to free him from 291 now circled in his mind. He marveled how chance happenings and uttered words could change everything. Suddenly, he had a plan. A very good plan. And Eric need not worry. The boogeyman wasn't getting him now or ever. It was the boogeyman who needed to be afraid.

TICK

Michael shoved his shoulder against the door. It gave up a groan as he flung it open and leaped from the car.

"Stop! Police!"

Of course, the dumbass kept running. And the perp sure could run. Michael wished he could avoid a foot pursuit because athletic ability had not been handed down to him in his DNA. Probably wasn't in his father's, either.

The guy had been moving from vehicle to vehicle in the lot, peering in windows, rattling the trunks and trying all the doors. Michael waited until he made an absolute move, figuring it wasted some shift time and would score him an incontestable arrest. The dimwit picked out a sparkly, new-looking, red sports Mazda coupe—like that wouldn't be hard to find—and, damn, if he wasn't lightning-quick getting into the vehicle.

He didn't look to be a professional though, more an opportunist taking advantage of a careless owner's absent-mindedness. It was surprising how many people neglected the simple action of pressing a lock button.

Michael should have moved more quickly. When he pulled his cruiser in front of the Mazda to block the thief, he hadn't anticipated him jumping over his hood. The Usain Bolt wannabe made it to the field behind the supermarket even before Michael had managed to leap from his car.

By the time he'd entered the jungle of dried grass and evergreen weeds, the guy was halfway across the expanse. The growth was above knee height and the ground uneven, and it was a struggle to get through the mess.

Oh, for a machete. And to be able to use it in more ways than were intended or legal if I catch this guy.

Then, as luck would have it, the asshole fell and disappeared below the green-yellow mass growing on the vacant lot. He must have tripped, or this was the worst attempt at hiding he'd ever witnessed.

"Now I got you," Michael said under his breath, as he lifted his knees higher, almost skipping through the brush. The owners of the vacant block needed a cleanup order to be issued. This was dangerous and not particularly helpful for pursuits. God knew what lurked there, too.

Before Michael could reach the man, he was up again but now seemed to limp with his first few steps. Michael was gaining on him and considered the sweet bliss of delivering an elbow to the asshole's head for making him run through this shit.

He began to smile and feel good about this making a great story to tell his dad when he felt his ankle twist beneath him as his foot landed on what must have been a large and uneven rock. At this running speed, he had no chance. He had only enough time to extend his hands to break his fall, so with zero grace, he hit the ground hard. A groan erupted from his mouth as the impact knocked the wind out of him.

He lay there panting before the thought of snakes and spiders crawling over him got him up in an instant. His hand sought his weapon as he scanned the field in case the asshole doubled back. Frank Chester's story swirled in his head as he checked that he still had his pistol. He did.

His training officer's voice pinged him: *stay alert and be prepared for attack.* In this instance, it was a wasted lesson as Mr. Bolt had done what all cockroaches do on instinct: scuttle away at light speed.

"Fuck you," he said, not just to the escaped moron but to the careless owner who'd allowed this patch of land to become so overgrown and treacherous. He'd certainly make some calls back at the station to the city council. Could be dead bodies in there for all anyone knew.

He began the trudge back to his car, careful not to place too much weight on his ankle. It didn't feel too bad but that could be the adrenaline. Of course, there was the 291 *Factor* to consider. Since he'd drawn the short straw again today, having been reassigned the hell-car, who knew what other misfortunes might befall him?

It was little wonder that he fell. Today had been a doozie. Only an hour ago, a pebble with 291's name on it had kicked up from a truck and cracked the windshield which meant he'd have to fill out more paperwork to get that repaired immediately. And the asshole computer had frozen, *again!* And, of fucking course, he *would* end up tripping while chasing a stupid perp, who was some track and field star, it seemed. All he needed now was a flat tire to underline the day as 291's version of perfect.

He dusted off his pants, his palms brushing in a firm stroke across the material to remove the grass seeds which clung there like white-green fleas.

As he neared 291, he couldn't help himself; his foot kicked out and connected hard against the tire. Despite the jarring he received, it felt so good that he struck out again. This time, his aim collided with the front fender.

This one hurt and made him angry.

"Fuck you. Happy now, bitch?"

All he wanted was to get home, down a couple of beers and sleep off this wreck of a day. He stood beside his enemy, staring across the field with one thought running through his mind: please God, let tomorrow be better!

Later, as he was enjoying a hot-as-he-could-handle shower, washing the day's crap from his body, he saw something that made him sick. He realized in that moment that this whole thing with the car had become deadly serious.

Just below his knee, there protruded a little black ball. Correction: a dark red and black ball. At first, he thought it was dirt. But he was wrong. It was a very alive and disgusting tick. A dirty, goddamned tick!

Oh, what a big mistake he'd made in not tucking his pants inside his socks before running through the grass. But it wasn't as if he had a world of time to think through his next move.

Screw this!

Now he would need to fill out an injury report, just in case he ended up with Lyme disease. God, he hoped he didn't end up with that horrible illness. If it became serious, at least the job's insurance would cover him. But with 291's curse following him everywhere, he stood a solid chance of having his leg amputated and the insurance company suddenly finding a get-out clause.

It's hardly the vehicle's fault, he reasoned. A car didn't have the power to call forth insects to attack him as in an Egyptian mummy's curse.

Still, the feeling that something watched while playing with him, and enjoyed his distress, prickled at the nape of his neck. When he climbed out of the shower, he didn't even wait to towel himself dry. He immediately grabbed tweezers from the medicine cabinet because now he'd seen it, he felt sick. Whether due to the concept of a thing sucking on him or the normal progression of a bite, the skin throbbed around the area where the bloodsucker protruded.

After the bug's bulging body was in the tweezer tips, he eased out the little monster with great care. Once free, he held the insect up to the bathroom light and shivered seeing its legs wriggle as it fought for life. The thing had tried to eat him alive—just like the other parasite which lived and thrived inside the wires and metal of 291.

Michael pulled the still-kicking creature from the tweezer and clasped its swollen form between his thumb and forefinger. Then, with great pleasure, he squeezed. More blood than he could have believed a small insect could hold, burst forth in a mini-explosion and slithered down his fingers. Satisfaction flooded through him at exterminating the intruder with such a simple gesture.

That was what he needed to do with 291. *Squeeze the life out of it!* No more waiting. He'd fight back, once and for all because things didn't look as though they'd right themselves on their own. Life didn't work that way. Well, his life anyway. No happy ending coming for him. Nobody to save him. This was him going to hell in a hand-basket or, more accurately, a cruiser. He would need to work this one out for himself. And he'd just begun to realize how.

If they didn't allocate him 291 tomorrow, he'd request the car. Knowing his luck, the day he wanted it would be the day they gave him another one. But no matter what happened, the evil flowing through the thing would be stopped. Finito. Sayonara. Goodbye. After this was over, he'd quit the force—and who would blame him?

He flicked the tick's remnants into the toilet bowl and flushed. Then he washed his hands more than necessary, before climbing into bed and sleeping the sleep of the dead.

GIFT

For all Michael's bravado of the night before, his determination was paper thin. He'd always struggled with sticking to things, having played on so many different sporting teams during school that he'd been nicknamed *The Spare*. He was *not bad* at most things but an expert at none. His favorite color had changed so many times during his childhood that his room looked like a kaleidoscope. And as for the food he loved; that changed daily.

He thought that in becoming a cop, this personality flaw might be fixed. Well, look how well that had gone!

So here he sat, in his *favorite* car, thinking hard if today might *not* be the best day to fight back. Of course, he hadn't needed to request 291 because he'd been given it, yet again. They kept booking it out to him as if the two were partners.

Michael's mind was flitting everywhere as he stared out across the river. There was something mesmerizing about the water eddies. The way they joined, swirling around each other before separating, only to repeat the whole thing again as if involved in an intricate, choreographed dance. It seemed pointless because they ended up in the same place, flowing into the unknown, none of them masters of their destiny.

His thoughts took that visual and applied it to his situation. If he didn't take control, there was his future. Just like his father's life—expending pointless amounts of energy to do nothing more than whirl around in circles with no chance of avoiding the inevitable. Death, taxes and 291.

His mind was a rubber band wrapped over a pulley. Every time the demon car did something to him, a cog turned another notch and stretched him closer to the breaking point before easing backward just enough that he doubted himself. And let's face it, the next step he'd contemplated only twenty-four hours prior, was a hell of a leap.

But something had been working its way inside his lack of resolve since he'd awakened this morning, especially after the *tick incident*.

He'd suddenly realized it wasn't only his life and health at risk. His family was also in danger.

Two days ago, his mother had cut herself with a box knife within an hour of him visiting. She'd only mentioned it when he'd told her about the tick. "Didn't want to alarm you, honey," she'd said. While opening yet another delivery from Amazon—an addiction, Michael had begun to suspect—she'd explained that her hand had slipped. A visit to emergency and four stitches later, she was okay. But his mom had said something very alarming. She admitted to feeling a force pushing her fingers.

"I'm just being silly," she said when Michael had asked her to explain what she meant.

He didn't need an explanation though. He knew this was no accident. It had to be tied to this haunting... possession... ghost-slash-demon-asshole thing which had attached itself to his life. No other explanation made an ounce of sense. He'd done nothing to deserve this, yet here he was starring in his own Amityville Horror story on wheels.

If something did happen to his family and he could have prevented it, he couldn't live with himself. He'd moved back in with his folks after his marriage had ended. At first, he felt embarrassed but as he saw it, living with them had been one of the pros—besides getting away from the biggest mistake of his life.

It stopped his mom nagging him to come visit, for one thing. Now, he enjoyed a home-cooked meal, his bed made and his clothes washed as if he was fifteen again. If he was being honest, the food was the biggest bonus.

The con was that though he loved his mom and, he guessed, his dad too—though sometimes he wondered—they could both get under his skin, his mother with her over-fussing and his dad with his unvoiced, unfulfilled expectations.

Michael could sometimes tell by the roll of the man's eyes exactly what he was thinking: *you're a disappointment, son. But why did I expect anything more?*

This supposed accident of his mom's seemed more like a warning from his tormentor. *You play with me, I play with you. Not just you, my friend, but anyone you love.*

It made him see his parents as vulnerable pawns in this power struggle. The truth of it hung before him, flapping its taunting, raggedy shreds. His job, which saw him running across rocky fields chasing perps, speeding after dangerous drivers, always placing himself in harm's way every shift, was a fool's game.

Well, that was an exaggeration of course because those incidents hadn't been the norm. Still, real danger was probably coming for him just like in *Law and Order*.

And what did he expect to receive for this heroism?

A comfortable retirement?

An award for his mantlepiece?

Friendship that would last a lifetime?

Nope, nah, not a chance.

How many cops you ever hear saying they're comfortable and happy in their golden years and still keep up with their work buddies with whom they've shared decades of great memories? That didn't happen either if his dad was a case in point.

The future looked more like the rust-bucket years filled with financial struggles, plus physical pain from on-the-job injuries and emotional issues after dealing with the lowest forms of humanity day in, night out. He really should have stuck to security. No blood-sucking creatures living in those gated communities, well, none from the insect world.

Added to that soggy mess of an average cop's life, was his very own *Christine*. Vehicle 291, that haunted motherfucker.

He'd be crazy as a loon to spend another second *faithfully and impartially executing the duties of his office as a law enforcement officer according to the best of his skill, abilities and judgment; so help him, God.*

Seemed God wasn't keen on offering Michael any help, and this thing had gotten so out of hand it was now well beyond his abilities to solve. The snapping band twanged in his head, cracking his mind into decisions, decisions. Yes, he'd decided a handful of times what to do—but imagining it and then carrying it out lay on different sides of the fence. This attack on a person he loved though... now that crossed a line.

A little sneaking hope tugged at him. Once this was done, and he revealed the fight he'd undertaken to his dad, the older man might just view his son in a new light, congratulate him on the iron balls it had taken to do this and possibly save other cops too, rookies such as him who wouldn't have had the courage to act.

"Hey, Mike," he imagined his dad saying, even if he wouldn't manage to look him in the eyes as he did so. "Mike, I'm proud of you, son."

His mom had once shared the depth of his father's pride; at the swearing-in ceremony, she'd said, Dad had even shed a couple of tears. The last time that had happened, she assured him, was at his own dad's sister's wedding. Just typical. His aunt only needed to say *I do* in a pretty dress. However, he was required to put his life on the line to get even a smidgen of emotional response from his dad. The guy was always about business.

"Don't you get too ahead of yourself. Long road. Looong, bumpy road." Those had been his encouraging, congratulatory words.

Fantastic! Thanks so much, Dad. That really motivates me.

Well, this would become the day he'd prove something to himself and to the world. As he completed the last few hours of his final shift, he repeated each step of what he thought of as his *fluid* plan. The thought that—very, very soon— 291 would pay dearly for all the aggravation, filled him with a sense of euphoria.

No. More. Bullshit... Not on his watch.

He'd already started the ball a-rollin'. Calling in to Headquarters ten minutes ago, he'd started putting the steps together. Not everything had been worked out, but he was confident, somehow, that things would slot into place. It was the force of his will that would win out.

"Nauseous. Can't keep a thing down. Food poisoning from a bad burger," was the excuse he'd given for needing to abandon his shift early. "Don't think I can make it to the swap-over for vehicle changeover. I'll return the car to the precinct."

His strategy was to stay close to help, in case anything went wrong, and this swap-over location was too far away from where he needed to be.

These meet-up locales were spread throughout the city, and it was his dumb luck that today's spot was not the most suitable for his plan.

"Hell, gotta have cars all over the fucking city," was the response when he asked why they changed shifts out in the streets. "We need 'em standing by, geared up, poised at the ready, just in case something big goes down. Can't have dozens of vehicles trying to get out from the precinct all at once."

So, he must play the hand he was dealt, with this swap point being in the wrong place, and he figured pretending he was sick wasn't half bad.

Other than being unwell, which would add to the legitimacy of what came next, records would show his behavior was not out of the ordinary. He didn't anticipate things going awry, but you never knew, especially when dealing with 291.

Always be prepared hammered around inside his head. That drove him nuts too. He'd be beyond pleased to have that mantra fade away. Once the dust settled over what was about to happen to him, nobody could possibly blame him for quitting. It was perfect. So, so perfect.

He imagined his mother's face as her palms cupped his cheeks. "Nothing's worth your life. You'll be just as happy working in an office or doing something with your hands. Your dad and I don't want you back there placing yourself at risk."

Fucking sweet!

A radio squawk interrupted his thoughts, an assault and robbery at an ATM. He considered ignoring it. After all, he had the perfect excuse having reported being sick. Problem was though, he was literally a block away and the closest, and it sounded a little exciting. If he didn't want to throw any suspicion on himself, he should respond. In fact, that would make him look even more the hero.

Surely it wouldn't delay him for too long because the perp would be long gone if he drove slowly.

He picked up the mic and pressed the speak button.

"291 to Headquarters, I'll take the two-four-one."

"Headquarters 291. Copy that. Thank you. Perp described as five-six, dark hair, wearing a green t-shirt and jeans."

"291 Headquarters. Copy description. On my way."

Michael pulled the wheel hard, the tires screeching as the cruiser turned and headed back in the direction he'd just driven.

He'd only traveled three hundred yards when he caught sight of a man running along the sidewalk, his head twisting around to check the street behind. Green t-shirt and jeans... check. And looking as guilty as any dumbass who didn't have the sense to use a getaway vehicle or find a backstreet.

This one really was stupid because when he saw the cop car, instead of bolting, he stopped, even paused for a few seconds to look up and down the road. Then, as if someone had whispered in his ear that he'd better run, he finally swung around and took off in the opposite direction to which he'd been running.

He was much slower though. Must have exhausted his turbo-speed absconding from the ATM. In a dramatic move, Michael swung hard around and bumped the car up and over the curb in front of the guy. He expected him to continue to run, like the one back at the store lot who ran off through the field. This moron, however, was far more obliging. He simply stopped dead and looked terrified.

Michael leaped out, gun drawn and realizing why the presumed perp had put up such little effort. He couldn't have been more than fourteen or fifteen, a baby-faced teenager.

"Stop. Police. Hands up and behind your head."

He'd miss saying that. So Law and Order.

"Turn 'round. Down on the ground. Lie flat. Hands where I can see them, to the side of your head, or you'll be sorry."

The kid followed his directions as if he was the star of a *Simon Says* game. He didn't even brace himself to avoid hitting his chin on the pavement as he obediently locked his fingers behind his neck.

Within thirty seconds, the pathetic excuse for a robber had been handcuffed and Michael was searching him. Three hundred in crisp, new notes were shoved in his jeans' back pocket.

"This yours?" he said waving the notes by his face.

His captive didn't reply.

"Nothing to say? Then, I'll answer for you. I don't think so. We'll just go talk to the real owner, shall we?"

He pulled the trembling kid to his feet and marched him toward the car. For a moment, he considered including him in the coming events, somehow. His initial exhilaration at collaring him with ease had taken him off track and messed with the next step. This was what happened when you didn't stick to your plan. Darn, now he was having buyer's remorse. He should never have responded to the call. It was always going to affect his timing. He wished he'd *stayed alert* on his own plan!

A whisper of a breeze slipped across his face as he paused at the rear door contemplating this SNAFU. Was that feeling not the wind after all, but a warning? The finger of fate reaching out telling him to back the fuck off?

"Oh shit," he muttered, as he pushed the young criminal into the vehicle, his palm planted on the top of his head. He was allowing fear to invade his mind. Of course, the kid couldn't be with him when it happened because something might go wrong, and he had no intention of killing anyone by accident. Besides, figuring how to set the whole thing in motion with company in tow was beyond his current mental capacity. Too much was happening that he hadn't factored in, with so much at stake.

The boy refused to speak even when he Mirandized him. Instead, the teenager nodded, his eyes bright with adrenaline. His shaking hands answered Michael's next question, but Michael was asking it anyway because he loved this part. Whenever the opportunity arose, he delivered it with gusto as if a camera was zoomed in for a closeup.

"Hey, kid, you gotta ask yourself one thing? *Do I feel sorry?* Well, do ya, punk?"

It was his version of a Clint Eastwood *Dirty Harry* line. But instead of *lucky*, he inserted *sorry*, making it his own original. He liked this saying better than, "Go ahead, make my day."

"Well, do ya, punk?" he repeated.

Still no reply.

"Okay then, you can answer me at the station," Michael said as he shoved the boy into the backseat, still careful to push his head down as he bent to slide inside.

As he climbed behind the wheel, he suddenly realized the size of his problem. He couldn't just drop the kid off and hope someone else would deal with him. This was not a misdemeanor and would require him to be interviewed and booked. How long that'd take, especially if this wasn't his first offense, Michael didn't know. He'd have to speak to the victim too. Quite possibly, they'd hold a lineup. Then he'd need to file a report.

Fuck!

Through all this, he would need to ensure his behavior was of someone who was feeling very unwell.

Then it struck him. This was, in fact, a gift. He'd be seen at the precinct by many there and could feign exhaustion. What about making himself throw up in the bathroom? Unappealing, yes, but certainly convincing.

Later, when questions were asked, there'd be witnesses to attest to how sick he appeared. This then would make it very conceivable that he would take a different route to the swap zone. He'd simply say he passed out and remembered nothing. When it was over, he'd become a double sympathetic figure: a dedicated officer who'd carried on despite being so unwell.

I'll be a hero. A fucking hero!

He chuckled and shook his head in a triumphant slow shake, unable to believe his good fortune at this turn of events. Things had shaped up to perfection. This proved, without a doubt, he was indeed on the right track. Luck had finally smiled upon him.

So, fuck you, haunted car.

SICK

Michael checked his gun into the locker outside Interview Room 3. Whenever an officer or detective questioned a suspect, they were required to lock their firearm away before entering, then pick it up once done. Every interview was recorded, and this also played into his plan.

He entered the small room—dimensions on TV shows were a wild exaggeration—and made his shoulders noticeably droop. Placing a palm on his chest, he rubbed in a circular motion as if suffering heartburn.

The boy was only thirteen, as it turned out, and shit scared. He had the wild-eyed look of a trapped animal that knew its days were numbered. Thanks to his age, he'd receive nothing more than a slap on the wrist. Such a small deterrent against future crime, which Michael imagined would give the boy permission to work his way up to bigger and better things. Maybe he'd hit the jackpot next outing, with armed robbery.

Just like me in a funny way.

He too would shortly end up doing something bigger and better than battling a demon car and the flawed system would be responsible for his predicament.

He grimaced, not because he wasn't happy at the thought, but because it was part of his convincing performance. The kid must have taken the expression for a smile because he returned a nervous grin. Perhaps the boy was thinking Michael's apparent illness might lessen the charges. Maybe he imagined he might be let off with a simple warning.

Well, he could be in luck. Not only was Michael about to conduct the weakest interview ever, but his plans did not include more than a few questions. If that.

As he warmed to the whole idea, he hammed up his performance. Not too much, but just enough so that anyone who was watching or replaying the recording would feel for a fellow officer suffering nausea and severe discomfort. He had no intention of carrying on the pretense longer than necessary though.

He threw a few questions at the kid, which he finally answered. This one had no record and looked ready to burst into tears. After being so quiet earlier, he seemed happy replying to everything asked of him.

Name. Address. Where had he been that day? Nothing too difficult because, at the same time, Michael needed to focus on his acting skills. He rubbed at his temples and took several deep breaths, expelling air in short puffs through pursed lips, just like a woman in labor.

"Phaaah. Phaah. Phaah-fhooooh."

He exaggerated the last breath, so it sounded as if he'd neared the end of his self-control and was close to losing his breakfast, lunch and last night's dinner.

The kid furrowed his brows as he stared first at Michael, then around the room. He clearly wondered what he should do. Keep talking, offer help or just shut up?

"Oooh. Oh. Phaah."

Criminal Jr. squirmed in his chair and offered, "Are you okay, Sir?"

He may have imagined showing concern would score him

brownie points. A possibility, but that'd be up to whoever took over after Michael exited stage right.

Well here goes, he thought, as he reached down to clutch his stomach. A burp-come-growl erupted from his throat, and he winced as if kicked in the guts.

"Excuse me," he said, lolling his tongue out like a sick dog.

"Sir. All cool. If it's okay to say... you look terrible. Like, bad, dude."

Perfect. Thank you, kid!

If anything came up in the subsequent investigation, this would-be heister could speak to how ill he'd appeared.

How hilarious! A perp would be his witness!

Michael circled his other hand in the air while still clutching his middle.

"Oh, no," he gasped through clenched teeth, before covering his mouth. The boy's worried expression transformed into surprise. He was now expecting to receive a spray of vomit instead of questions.

"Be right..." Pause, for an exaggerated dry-retch. "Back."

Michael pushed his hands hard against the table's edge and shoved away. The chair's metal legs scraped and squealed across the floor. He stood, acting as if he was uncertain what to do next, before turning and taking three strides to the exit where he pretended to fumble with the lock.

Damn, he was Tom Hanks personified!

Once he stepped through the doorway, he headed straight to the Sergeant's office and knocked.

A gruff voice answered, "Yeah, come."

He pushed down on the handle and entered, but not before remembering to clutch at his stomach and strap a pained expression on his face.

"Sorry sir, but I'm not feeling so great. I got this perp in Interview Room 3... but I don't think I can continue. My shift's over in forty-five." He stopped here for a second to swallow, giving the impression he was near vomiting. He shook his head in obvious desperation and breathed a slow sigh. "If I leave now for the swap-over, that'd help. Please."

"You look like crap, Chambers. You're no use to us like this, officer. Go, get rest. Someone'll take over."

The Sergeant rose from behind his desk and maneuvered past him to the door. Michael followed as his boss took a few steps into the large room, where he stopped, hands on his hips, and surveyed the space. The place bustled with officers going about their jobs: they were seated at desks, on the phones or tapping away at computers. Others stood talking with colleagues. One female officer exclaimed, "Shit!" and then dabbed at a spilled coffee beside her laptop.

Michael's boss called out, "Selinski! You free?"

A heavy-set hulk of a human being with hooded eyes and thick, caterpillar-furry eyebrows, replied. "Can be, sir."

The Sergeant pointed toward the man. "Fill him in without throwing up everywhere, Chambers." Then he looked at Michael and added, "Get yourself better quick... and don't give it to anyone else on your way out!" before retreating into his office.

Michael took a few minutes to run through what he had on the kid. Selinski waved him away when Michael apologized for dry retching in his direction.

"No problem, buddy. You're only human."

"Thanks. All I'm thinking is that I need to collapse into bed."

This wasn't his thought, at all.

More lies.

He'd become talented at telling them and pretending. Maybe, he wondered, a career might lie ahead which utilized these skills? Car salesman? Real estate agent? Banker? Broker? There was money in sales jobs he'd read recently, with the economy on the up. But that was all cotton candy thinking because what truly filled his mind was his anticipation of the next thirty minutes and the incredible euphoria of his impending freedom.

RIVER

On the way to the car, Michael sent a text to Joe Carmen—the officer scheduled to take 291 after his shift—asking if they could move up their meeting? Within a minute, Joe had responded in the affirmative.

As Michael walked toward the lot, his confidence bloomed that his next calculated move was perfect. Yes, he was nervous, but the sense of impending finality spurred him on. This gave him a chance at a future. If he waited to see how things eventuated if he did nothing, who knew what might happen?

Only bad things, he told himself. *Only bad, rotten, scary things.*

His enemy sat awaiting, a wolf in steel clothing. The headlights caught the sun's reflection, making it appear as if yellow eyes watched and anticipated its quarry's approach.

He wasn't afraid of whatever had possessed the car anymore. Valor came from action. His belief in the necessity of escaping its jaws so strong, nothing could stop him. Angels surely rested on his side.

Throw hell at me, you monster. I'll meet you and raise you double.

He wished he had shared his plans with Eric, brought him in on the deal, but he feared implicating his friend when this was investigated. He'd seen him at the precinct earlier, standing by the water cooler, and he so wanted to stop and call him into the bathroom and spill his guts like an excited child. Though Eric had nodded and taken a step toward him, Michael had played an avoidance move, tapping at his watch to indicate he was running late and exiting quickly. Once enough time had passed, though, Michael would recount this crazy adventure over a beer.

As he pulled open the car door and slid inside, Michael inhaled deeply and soaked up the joy of perching on the edge of a win. He had some dollars saved from before he'd joined the force and he thought he'd take a vacation. *Somewhere in the sun.*

The Beach Boys had it right: West Coast girls with their suntans, and the drinks, palm trees and sand sounded pretty damned good right about now.

His phone buzzed. A return text from Joe Carmen appeared on the screen.

Be there in 5.

Officers usually met at a designated spot a half hour before shift end to change over vehicles, but this guy was doing him a solid. He didn't know the officer well, but guilt tapped at Michael that his colleague would be left waiting around for him as a no-show. Still, his annoyance would soon disappear once he heard what had happened.

He started the engine, and a thrill of satisfaction traveled through him as it roared into life. The thing living in this machine had no idea what was coming. Inside his head, though, a thick, dullness grew. Something pushed at him. Did it sense what he had in store?

Well, too late.

Unless it could control the brakes and steering—and so far, that hadn't happened—then this was a fait accompli.

He was mindful that the route to the swap-over point needed to appear logical for later questions. His actions must be plausible. Man, he was good at this. He'd thought of everything. He broke into his version of the familiar *Ghostbusters'* tune.

"Who ya gonna call? Yeah! De-mon Busters. Something strange... under the hood..."

Then he stopped singing and said to the cabin around him, "Officer Frank Chester, if it's you, please return to hell and take your ve-hi-cle with you. Or would that be vice versa? Your car can go to hell and take you too. Both of you can fuck right off, out of my life!"

Within ten minutes, his route had taken him alongside the river, approaching the same place where—only a day before—he'd hatched this idea.

The fact he'd been assigned 291 again today proved divine intervention was happening here.

"Bet you never imagined it'd be me," he said to nobody as he slowed the car to turn into Riverside Park's entrance. The gold-tipped ironwork fence and open gates reminded him of English castles and royal history. Well, history here he came.

An exit on the other side of the park, two miles away, would still have him headed in the swap-point's direction. His story that he felt sick and didn't even remember turning in here was reasonable.

This was a graceful, peaceful oasis cushioned against the river that flowed through the city. It was more than a century and a half old, a haven amid the towering urban surroundings. A walkers-and-cyclists-wide double pavement ran alongside the road. Thick, aged oaks, with gum trees dotted between, separated the glimpses of carefully-manicured open spaces and wandering paths. Mid-afternoon saw the park nearly empty, and that was perfect.

Another sign.

On his prior reconnaissance, he'd noted that two hundred yards farther along, the barrier of trees thinned to only thirty feet from the riverbank. The drop to the river here wasn't as high as elsewhere along this stretch; it was maybe only fifteen feet, with no rocks or ledge and just the dark depths waiting.

Somewhere, he had read an article saying this was one of the deepest rivers in the county, wide and deep and perfect for him.

He'd worked up a story which would fit pretty well.

All he could remember, he'd say, was that an animal—a dog perhaps—had run in front of his car. In a shaking voice, he'd explain how in his panic he'd hit the accelerator instead of the brakes. The last thing he'd fake recall was being flung from the car. And, *thank God*, he'd add. *Thank God.* He could have died.

The beauty of this awesome plan was that he could claim PTSD. After everything this haunted car had thrown at him, he didn't doubt he had a touch of it anyway. He'd extend the pretense by claiming a sweat-inducing fear every time he thought about getting into any vehicle resembling a cruiser.

Oh yeah, post-traumatic stress disorder was a get-out-of-jail-free card. He might even score a pension or compensation if things went well.

So, fuck the Department! Now they'd have to pay for his angst.

His chest tightened when he saw the lamp post up ahead, which he'd marked with duct tape. This signaled his take-off point, the marking big enough for him to see but too small for anyone else to notice.

No-one in sight still. Another sign from fate; every step of the way, she'd sent encouragement.

Michael Chambers, you're the man.

Yes, he was indeed. And he'd prove it in the next few seconds.

Can I do this? Can I really, really do this?

Yes, he could, and he would.

I'm the Demon-Buster guy.

Exhilaration gripped him, despite his out-of-control heart so close to exploding. His stomach churned like the river he'd soon face. He was a bigger hero than Frank Chester would ever be.

That idiot got himself killed but Michael wouldn't because he was a fighter. He'd stare in death's eye and survive to tell his children, and then his grandkids, about the day he destroyed the haunted car.

As the moment approached, everything slowed like the scenery was on a children's carousel rotating around him. He sucked in deep, lung-filling breaths and prepared. His fists clenched the wheel at positions three and nine as he flexed his elbows to brace. As his foot shoved down hard on the accelerator and the engine gunned, he held his breath. With a quick, determined action, he swung the car up and over the curb.

Beneath him, he felt a teeth-jarring bump, which threw him upward from his seat. A bang startled the hell out of him. Then the interior echoed with a horrible, metallic scraping noise as the cruiser's base dragged over the raised edge of the concrete sidewalk. Adrenaline flooded his body and his fingers shook. He paid little attention though because his focus was through the windshield and on those thirty feet he had yet to cover. Thirty feet to freedom.

For a micro-second, his thoughts switched to, *what the hell am I doing? Slam on the brakes and stop this craziness!*

He glanced at the speedometer, and the smart, confident voice that had come up with this plan answered back with the words he needed to keep going.

Too late for regrets, Officer Chambers. We're already at forty miles an hour. Enjoy the... riiiide!

But in the last split-second, something happened in his brain. Something like a freaky, electric misfire. If anyone asked him later why he did it, he couldn't begin to tell them.

His initial plan had been to open the door and roll out. The risk of a sprain or a few broken bones was all he anticipated. And if that happened, no problem, it would only add to his story of PTSD. So, bring it on. He'd run that move—of relaxing his body as he exited, and then rolling—through his head at least a dozen times. Practice made perfect, right?

Something caused him to hesitate. Fear of hurting himself or getting stuck halfway out and being dragged along, maybe? So that in the last split-second as he headed for the bank and the point of no return, the 'smart voice' screamed at him.

Why not, Michael? You can swim. More realistic. Less risk. In for a penny, in for a pound, buddy!

So, he went along with that because, really, who could argue with that kind of logic? And before he knew it, the time to rethink was over. He was in the air and riding a momentary magnificent arc over the water as if he was a police version of Evel Knievel or like one of those tough guys in *Fast and Furious.*

Fucking wow! Vin Diesel eat my dust.

Then the impact as the car hit the water; this now wasn't even close to the movies. He registered the splash as being bigger than he'd expected.

His head was thrown forward with such violence he thought it might fly off his neck and through the windshield, before it slammed back against the seat, hard... and his knee smashed into something solid and unforgiving.

The wheel? Car door? What the—?

Had he hit a motherfucking wall?

"Shit!" he screamed as an enormous wave engulfed 291; a tsunami, that's what it was, a freaking tsunami.

This was all he saw, before—

The airbag punched him in the face. And his chest. Not a soft pillow intent on saving his life. Not even close.

Christ, it hurt!

Then the white puffiness that covered him from waist to face, exploded with a boom as if someone had pricked the balloon. He thought he might have a heart attack from the shock.

Violent rocking became his world for longer seconds than he'd ever lived, as waves of water collided around the car's exterior. Now he knew how a sock in a washing machine felt. *Peachy to be alive* were not the words that sprung to mind.

His left wrist collided with a window. If any bones of it were broken, that was okay. Not his dominant hand anyway.

Good. I'm thinking clearly, he decided at the clarity of the thought. He needed his head screwed on because he'd have to swim, and this experience was a little more terrifying than rolling out of a door.

But time slowed, and his logical mind had returned. It had some questions.

Why'd you do that, Mikey? Why? You had a plan and now what you got? You're in trouble, boy.

And he answered himself.

Because I couldn't let that motherfucker beat me. I'll get out of this, just you see.

Then pinpoints of searing white lights, like dozens of stars, sparked in his vision. Just as quickly they faded to pink, blue and finally dark gray. Blackness flooded inside his mind and his vision as he began to lose consciousness.

Wait, was that a whisper coming from behind and above his ear? Someone leaning over from the back seat?

You're such a fool, Officer Chambers. Such a goddam fool.

Before he could reply, an intense shimmer of pure gold appeared through the windshield. He was awake now, at least he thought he was, as he pulled himself forward with a grip on the wheel to see what the thing was that came swimming toward him.

Coming for him?

As it grew nearer, the golden glow deepened and flowed around the car, a cover of shimmering iridescence.

"You're such a fool, Officer Chambers."

As if one with the voice, the glow swayed in time with the words. He did try to answer. *No, just desperate.*

But it remained unspoken on his tongue as everything faded to black—deep, endless black.

SODA

When he opened his eyes, police officer Michael Chambers didn't panic. The recognition and shock that things had spun out of control, hit him about the same time as the chill of the cold water swirling determinedly around his legs.

He was sinking downward, below the surface.

In training, they'd drilled them on how to stay calm, no matter the surprise you faced. During the lectures, his mind had wandered to the day he might face a madman carrying a weapon or happen upon an out-of-their-mind-batshit-crazy drug user. They'd given them the words to use and not use with someone threatening suicide —basically, anything that got your heart going and your mind racing. He'd run several speeches through his head about life getting better if you focused on the good stuff, specifically for this event.

Of course, they hadn't been briefed on what to do if you inherited a haunted car or flew off a riverbank in said *ve-hi-cle* and began sinking. He could certainly give great CPR if it happened to someone else and they got them out in time. His hope was whoever rescued him would have had the same training.

He was prepared for unexpected stress and being thrown in the deep end—literally that—but he'd lost precious time when he passed out. If he hadn't been so impulsive, he might have pre-planned what to do when he ended up in the river. That was him though, through and through. His personality, as his mom would say, was that of *a bull in a china shop*. "It'll be your undoing," came his mother's voice. He imagined the finger waggling that accompanied the message. And she might be right yet, but he prayed not. Her tear-streaked face popped in his mind when she heard what had happened.

He decided that now he didn't want his mom and dad to know the truth of this when he got out. His father wouldn't be proud and he'd definitely be disappointed to learn the lengths to which Michael had gone to extricate himself from what would seem to the old man to be a problem in his son's head. His dad could never comprehend why he hadn't asked his advice.

If his grandfather were still alive, he would be *turning over in his grave*, he imagined him claiming.

Too bad. They couldn't and shouldn't judge unless they faced the same dilemma. You see plenty as a cop, but haunted cars? Now that was pretty darn unique, even his dad would have to admit.

What about the positive? What about this being an example of his courage, of not settling, of thinking outside the box? What about it being a fine example of fighting back, even though he didn't know exactly what he fought against?

He'd work out what to say later, what story to spin.

The water had now risen to just below his waist.

And Jesus, it's freezing.

Already, his teeth had begun to chatter, and his mind felt sluggish like part of it was traveling away from him off into the depths. This must be how it felt just before you drowned, he thought, after the cold had set in and before the water dragged a man down.

And he oddly reminded himself that he knew just what to do for hypothermia, for a man dragged like a dead weight out of the water in the bitter cold of a black night. He thought about the aluminum foil blanket all nicely folded in the trunk, stored with other emergency supplies. Fat lot of use that blanket was; no way could he reach the trunk, and it'd be weighted down by the water even if someone else got there to reach the lifesaving stash.

He shoved the deflated airbag toward his feet and unbuckled his seatbelt before trying to open the door. While the handle worked fine, it was as if someone had propped a fridge against it.

Then he realized; to open it now was impossible. They'd taught him that, and it had stuck. The external and internal pressure needed to be equalized. For this to happen, the cabin must first fill with water.

He'd researched how to escape a sinking vehicle on Google when working out his plan. At the time, he'd decided it was too risky. Shame he hadn't reminded himself of this before he rammed the china shop.

Four minutes... That was how long the article said you had before your chance of survival became grim.

Three minutes before the car's electrics stopped working... all things being equal.

So, no big deal. *Stay calm, Michael, and do what you need.*

He needed to get a window down, take a deep breath, climb out and swim to the surface, which was not far away so far. The car wasn't fully submerged yet. He was soft around the stomach but still reasonably fit and, though his thumping heart reminded him his calm was clinging by a thin thread, his mind was still clear.

Here we go, he thought as he depressed the driver's window button and wondered why there wasn't the usual whirring sound.

Oh, because... fuck! Nothing.

He pressed again. This time harder. So hard that he jarred his finger.

"Ouch."

A whirring sound now came from inside the door but still, it didn't budge. This meant the mechanism worked, but for some reason, the window remained stubbornly immobile.

Oh, what a surprise for *heap-of-shit 291!* Why was he even expecting anything to work?

Concern slipped into his subconscious as a thread of calmness finally twanged apart and opened a floodgate of images, ones of drowning and horrific pain, of his poor mother crying over his grave, and of his father shaking his head, an arm tightly placed around her heaving shoulders.

"No, no, that's not happening," he shouted to himself as much as to the car. Right now, it was probably thinking it had won.

Maybe only *this* door had a problem?

He twisted around and leaned across the top of his seat to stare into the rear. No, the rear windows were smaller than the front, so they'd be the last resort to try. He really needed to move though. The water level had risen to begin lapping at the lower edge of the glove box.

Michael attempted to clamber over the center console in an awkward foot-first manner. The maneuver was made more difficult because his pants were wet and clinging, and he wasn't particularly flexible. The fitness tests they had to undertake every six months were okay and he'd imagined this would help him through, but—as he now became aware—the pathetic *beep test* hardly helped. No way did it simulate an ill-equipped officer with sodden pants and mild hypothermia trying to escape a shit-pit of a drowning vehicle that harbored a death-wish for its sole occupant.

Anyway, this was a stupid idea because he only ended up angled in an awkward leg-split over the computer screen. He didn't care if he knocked the electronic equipment askew as he struggled to get a limb into the footwell to give himself room, but the very mounting bracket he'd once complained about as *flimsy* was now going to prove stubbornly immobile. It was in on the death-wish. He was sure of it.

With a little back and forth rocking and repositioning, he finally managed to find his footing, although he was certain he'd pulled a hamstring quite severely. Even before he'd seated himself in the passenger seat, he had reached across to depress the window button.

His uncertainty kicked in again, uncertainty of the exactness of the theory that you have three minutes before the electrical systems short. Was it reliable anyway? But he surely had only seconds left, if that, even if it was accurate. *C'mon, you slow, fat fucker!* had become a chant in his head.

His fingers fumbled at this simple task because ice had now seeped into his core. Mixed with the racing adrenaline—because really, despite the cold, he was losing his cool—his hands and legs shook like he suffered Parkinson's.

Finally, Jesus, finally, he got his body and wayward digits to do what he needed of them. Something so simple, *just press the shitty button. Press it! Press it, you useless fucker!*

Whhhrrrr. Whirrr. Griwiiiiir.

Again, the whirring sound but no movement.

Not even half an inch.

Same as the other.

The gear mechanism refused to catch. Refused over and over.

What would cause that? Not the impact, surely? Not on both windows?

"Shit! Shit!"

He slammed his fist against the window. Stupid. Now his whole hand hurt and not just his finger.

It's okay. It's okay. Stay calm.

His head flicked around to stare into the rear area. He'd give that a try now. So, he pulled out his shirt to give himself more flexibility and maneuvered his body through the gap between the seats.

Again, he fought limbs that seemed to be playing for the other side. But somehow, by kneeling this time on the center console, he was able to throw himself onto the bench seat.

The grimy, oil-slicked water was staring him in the face, the stench of acrid, mostly stagnant fluids accosting his nostrils as he pushed and flailed onto the backseat.

He jammed a thumb onto the window button and this one landed straight and true. This time, his expectations were lower, but he hoped. God, he hoped as he'd never hoped before.

Nothing.

Oh no... fucking, pissing hell!

He felt weak now, too. The air in the small, humid space was depleting rapidly and his head felt heavy as if he might pass out. But he mustered all his remaining strength and shuffled across to the other window and—

Whhhrrrr. Whirrr. Griwiiiiir.

Of course, the windows in the rear weren't working. 291 was enjoying its final shot. The car was laughing at him, deep, throaty, evil, laughs.

He willed his breathing to slow, to take in oxygen and allow his brain to think, to plan, to save himself.

Okay, this hadn't gone as expected, but that was fine because he had one more trick up his sleeve. With even more of a struggle because of the computer and electronics, he wiggled back into the front passenger seat. More room this side without a steering wheel.

He shoved back in the seat and rolled to his left to reach behind for his gun. As he rolled, his head stooped lower, close—so close—

to the ever-rising surface of the stinking water.

He could see the oily slime working its way toward his nose and mouth. He could smell it. How long would it take to drown in that? How would that gas and water mix feel when it flooded the lungs? Would it burn? The waters were rising all the time.

He'd have one chance to grab the gun and shoot out the windshield. That should have been his initial move instead of this climbing around gig he'd embarked upon.

Not thinking right, boy, he heard his dad say. *Get the brain in gear, if you got one.*

"Yeah, well, see how well you'd do under these circumstances," he replied.

In his panic—and he would admit the stay-calm training was no longer working—his hand fumbled on the holster catch. He took three frustrating tries to release it. But it worked. *Thank God, it worked.*

"Ah, Jesus, no!"

His heart banged, fit to explode because the grappling, stiff fingers discovered nothing but an empty, hollow pouch.

His options had dwindled to none and his mind struggled to understand how or why. He stared out into the beams of yellow light stretching into the dark swell. The headlights had automatically switched on as the sensors registered the darkness of the surrounding depths, the car starting to sink.

He couldn't even understand why he was sinking. Surely, the air pocket should keep him afloat? But he knew shit about physics, so thinking about that now was a waste of valuable seconds. He'd Google it later when he got out of this.

Yeah, stay positive. Later...

Where the hell was his weapon? He'd never had a chance to even draw the thing and the one time he needed it... *Jesus!*

Then, in his mind's eye, he saw himself placing the gun in the locker outside the interview room. They were told to always leave keys as well to prevent this exact occurrence—forgetting your gun. Such a simple thing; if he'd left his keys, he'd have remembered. His preoccupation with playing sick had messed with his pea-brained head.

Fuck, fuck, fuck.

He was sinking quicker now, the air depleting to a point where there wasn't enough to keep the car near the surface much longer. He had to contact someone and tell them what had happened. Maybe they could do something or offer another idea of how to escape, his own version of *Apollo 13*.

He'd just use his cell.

Then his hopes sank because that would be the phone in his pants' pocket, the same pocket submerged in water risen to his waist. Yeah, and he didn't need to check if it still worked. He'd washed two cells so far and the survival rate had been nil.

Okay, Plan A, escaping, was a fail.

Plan B, the phone, was a soggy mess.

He leaned to the right and grabbed the radio mic. Why he hadn't done this first was beyond him. The electrics' life was three minutes, remember, and he was well past that. The headlights still glowed so Plan C it must be.

He depressed the talk switch and spoke, keeping his voice controlled—which showed his mental toughness, considering. The mind video of him recounting his story of bravery in facing death shone brightly to him, even under these circumstances. He was thinking *later* and that was a good thing. *When you don't give up, anything's possible.*

"291 to Headquarters."

Precious seconds slipped by as Michael sat waiting and shaking, thinking it could not be possible that even the radio didn't work. Then the operator answered, and he breathed a long sigh; all the horror and frustration of his circumstance exhaled in that one breath.

"Headquarters to 291, go ahead."

"291, I'm... in trouble. Officer requires urgent help—"

"Headquarters to 291, please explain the trouble and assistance required."

He gave up on call protocol when he struggled to press the button because of his shaking hand.

"Crashed into the river. Car's sinking. Fast. I went in about one mile inside Riverside Park. About five minutes ago."

He realized the air sounded dead with that dampened lack of echo coming from the microphone, which meant he wasn't transmitting. The on-light still glowed, but he began to panic.

Then she was back. His heart slowed again.

"Headquarters to 291. Say again. You broke up. Did you say, *crashed into the river*? Please confirm."

He depressed the mic button.

"Yes, that's affirmative. One mile inside—hello? Hello? Headquarters? You there?"

Again, the dead, thick air and this time, the lights were gone on the transmitter. In the last thirty seconds, the water had climbed a few inches past its base and he hadn't realized.

Shorted.

He banged his fist against the side of the radio.

The demon was winning. Frank Chester must be having the time of his death. Michael felt the malevolence watching, laughing, breathing, its hatred stinking up the remaining air in the cabin. He had dared to fight back, and now it had come for him.

What had it expected? That he lay down and die? Now the damned asshole thing was so near to winning—but still, it played with him. Before swinging the knockout punch, it would first torture him with hope as each avenue of escape closed.

"Shit."

The word escaped his lips as the knowledge hit him. He'd so foolishly placed himself in the worst position, trapped inside his enemy, Ahab swallowed by Moby Dick, sinking with no way out.

He slammed a clenched fist against the side window.

Fuck, that hurt.

He tried the window buttons again. Still not working.

Curling his body into a ball, as much as he could in such a confined space, he leaned back and brought his legs up and over the dash, before landing a heavy kick on the windshield.

Then again. Over and over.

His knees cracked and his muscles flinched with each impact, but he continued anyway until he couldn't take the pain anymore.

Same result. Nothing moved or broke or gave an inch. The pressure from outside was too great, his action akin to kicking a double brick wall. If he kept this up, he'd end up with broken ankles. Just his luck, the glass would break but he'd be too injured to swim to the surface.

He thought about climbing into the rear and trying to shove his way into the trunk and retrieve the tire iron. That option though, with the water risen so high and continuing to fill even quicker, would use too much of his diminishing time.

Think, Michael, think.

A minute or so was all he had, if that.

The glove box!

They kept the vehicle and emergency procedure manuals in there. Plus... how could he have forgotten, for Christ's sake? A multipurpose tool for cutting seatbelts! Hell, he could use that. How obvious! Pry open something! Jam it into the windshield, make a crack. Kick that crack wider. Yes, it was hopeful.

The glovebox was nearly submerged now but he grasped the catch and tugged. It surprised him how easily it came open. He couldn't see inside well with the dark and the water but he felt around with frantic fingers. There was no tool and no manuals, which took him a moment to register because that shouldn't have been the case.

They were in there before he went in for the interview with the kid thief. He'd opened it and even considered leaving his gun in there, so he wouldn't have to put it in the locker. Now, it was empty, except for something that wrapped around his fingers.

And what the hell was it?

It was a single sheet of paper which, still stuck to his fingers, he retrieved and held in front of his face.

There were hand-written words on it but the ink had run and he struggled to make it out.

Something about *Rookie*, and *call me* and was that *Eric* at the bottom? His friend Eric? But why would he leave a note in Michael's glove box?

The rest was nothing but a blurred mess, disintegrating as he moved the scrap to try and decipher more.

What was going on here?

He felt confused like you do when waking from a vivid nightmare where it takes a moment to realize it wasn't real, that you're safe. Except he wasn't safe, and this was still a nightmare.

It hit him then as he dropped his fingers and the mushy paper into the bitter cold water which was now lapping over the top of the dash. He wasn't getting out of here. 291 had won. 291 had fucking won.

Michael leaned back in his seat and looked up at the ceiling of the car. He was thinking, with surprising calm, that this will be the last thing he would ever see as he sucked at the last mouthfuls of air left: the roof of the thing he hated most in the world

That's when he saw the edge of the paper poking out from the sun visor. Again, he had the itchy feeling that he'd missed something important because that wasn't there before. He remembered pulling the visor down to practice his *sick* look just before he'd picked up the teller-machine thief. Nothing there then.

He reached up and slid the slip out, careful to hold it at the edges, so that his wet fingers didn't do any damage. His hands shook as he drew it closer to his face to stare at the words written across the page.

It took him three read throughs before it sank in. When it finally did, he screamed, "No way! No way this is real," as he banged palm against his forehead.

Yet, he saw it clearly now as he thought back to all the times 291 had taunted him. The flat spare tires. Scrambled computer. Dead battery. Lights not working. Even the current defective window switches, which should have worked because he still had power.

He ran everything that had happened through his head and, of course, there was a reason he'd got stuck with this demon so often. How stupid of him not to realize when at least twenty cars were always available on rotation!

He recalled the mocking smile of Pezzullo when he logged out 291 to Michael. Like the Stephen King book, *Christine,* he'd said.

The way his colleagues kept their distance but the sniggers he caught as he walked past them. Of course!

He thought back to Eric so easily believing the possession story and then convincing him for certain the car was indeed haunted. What did he say? That the same thing had happened to a guy called Jokelini? Jokelini... how had he not seen it?

That was all about this?

It was a big, fat, dumb joke.

He'd thought they were just a bunch of unfriendly assholes. How could he know they were enjoying themselves at his expense? Hey, if he'd been in on it, he might have done the same.

But he wasn't in on it.

He *was* the joke. Except the joke was on them because he'd believed it and taken action. He bet they hadn't expected that. Now, they'd have to live the rest of their lives knowing what they did.

Haze me at your own peril! he thought.

Michael peered through the windshield into the blue-black murk glowing eerily from the headlights' illumination. The car was tilting further downward as the weight of the engine dragged it into a thirty-degree angle. The surface was gone from his vision.

He felt the biting cold seeping into his body as the water rose higher and moved halfway up his chest. Whirlpool currents swam around him.

Man, it's freezing, fucking hell freezing.

Would the electrics cease before his life? He'd like to let Google know the three-minute sinking estimate wasn't so accurate. He must have been down here a good four or five. In the end, it didn't matter, it all amounted to not enough time. Not enough time to think through another plan, to say goodbye or to even say a prayer to a God he didn't believe in, especially after this.

Would he die in total darkness? These were the pressing questions now. Today was to have been his last shift as a cop, this accident his excuse for leaving the force. This had been meant to save him, not end him.

At least he'd go knowing that monsters from hell did not exist. Correction, they did but they lived inside human beings, as flesh and blood men with a sick sense of humor.

They were about to get their punishment in spades. He wondered if he could find a way to preserve the note. So when they found the car and his body, they'd realize how their sabotage had gone so very wrong. In his mind, he saw his backpack in the rear seat.

Yes, that could be his final move in this game.

With poor coordination—his tired, strained muscles—no longer his to command—he twisted around and leaned over, reaching down and feeling beneath the water. His hand found a strap of the wet canvas bag and, with a grunt, he heaved through the top of the seat gap and into the front.

He dragged the zipper across the opening and reached inside, searching through the contents until he found the half-full soda bottle. He unscrewed the lid, put the lip to his mouth and swallowed the contents, before shaking the last drops into the surrounding water. Holding it up, he checked and figured it was as empty as it was going to be, before shoving the note inside.

Then he twisted the cap back on tight, really giving it a shove at the end to be sure. He unbuttoned his shirt and placed the receptacle against his chest and pulled the material together again before rebuttoning. It took several tries for each button because his hands shook as if he'd been shocked with a taser.

It was so, so cold and that was a bitch. He didn't want his last thoughts to be whining about the cold. His eyes closed, and he tried to focus on his mom and his dad and how many times they'd told him they loved him. And how sorry he was that he hadn't been the son they deserved and hadn't made his father proud.

The chill seemed to be dissipating and he imagined the water eddies carrying him away. He even smiled as he willed that those involved read his message and found themselves cursed. Maybe they'd turn a different cruiser into a memorial car for him, and he'd come back and haunt the son-of-a-bitch unfortunate enough to be allocated it.

The words scrawled on the page danced in his mind. Michael smiled because it *was* kind of funny, that is if you ignored his impending death.

Happy Rookie Day, Chambers,

You've passed your initiation and survived the "haunting of 291." We have taken control of your windows, possessed with the help of your local squad mechanic. Call me and we'll come free you. Drinks on us to thank you for the laughs.

Eric and your grateful colleagues.

As the water rose higher, he coughed out a laugh. What can you say to that? Touched by the irony of the situation, his voice quavered, but there was no bitterness there because, hey, no doubt, Eric and his *colleagues* would be the haunted ones now.

"You're welcome, assholes... you're welcome."

December 2018

Loved 291?

Grab two **FREE** books by Susan May www.readerlinks.com/l/490258

After, please return here to turn the page and read Susan's popular *From the Imagination Vault,* where readers are taken behind the story to discover the inspiration for her stories.

After the Thank You section keep reading to enjoy a preview of The Troubles Keeper.

FROM THE IMAGINATION VAULT

Destination Dark Zone was to be about cleaning out my hard-drive of unfinished stories and sharing them with you. So, five re-invented tales from the last few years and, in the case of *Lucky This Time*, even decades past. But I wanted to write something new too.

Writers are always asked where they get their story ideas. Many times, I'll reply, "From listening and watching people." Then I'll add, "Be careful what you say. I might put you in a story and kill you." Oddly, most people have replied with great enthusiasm that they'd love to meet a violent end in one of my tales.

Before 291 drove into the slot, I was hunting for a set-up, as I call my ideas. Maybe something in the *Best Seller* world because readers had been asking for more. Or, what about exploring an alien invasion concept I'd had in the back of my mind for years? A few other notions floated around but I wasn't feeling the energy that always tells me *this is the one*.

Then I was messenger-chatting with Diane Lynch, my friend and wonderful moderator of my Facebook group Susan Mayhem Gang. Her husband is a retired New York Police Department officer and her son had just graduated.

She told me how the new graduate was having a bad week. His

computer had broken down, his car got a flat and he'd just found a tick in his leg from chasing a criminal through long grass. I offered my sympathies and suggested the car might be possessed. "You know, like *Christine*," I said.

It hit me right then as I typed those words that this was a great premise. So, it took me a couple of soaks in the bath, would you believe, to come up with the concept that the car wasn't possessed at all but part of a hazing initiation.

Diane then shared photos of her son and the police car he drove. It was a memorial vehicle, although the tragedy surrounding the police officer's passing was not the same as Frank Chester's. That scene was inspired by an actual crime I discovered during story research.

Diane passed on her husband Pete's sound suggestions on procedures whenever I asked. For instance, I needed to remove Michael's gun from his possession or he could easily shoot his way out of the sinking car. Pete explained interview procedures and sent pictures of the lockers outside interview rooms.

Pete also sent me several pieces of key information about panic buttons on the personal radio that members of the public wouldn't know about, but cops certainly would. He also shared some amusing stories.

To Pete and Diane, thank you for your help and kindness. Thanks go to your son as well for accidentally inspiring this story through his week of bad luck because I sure had a blast writing *291*.

And here's another thought… it may all seem like good fun playfully teasing others, having a great time at someone else's expense—such harmless behavior because everyone does it or has had it done to them.

The person who is the brunt of the joke might even appear to be enjoying the attention, but you never know where it'll all end up. Just sayin'.

January 2019

DESTINATION DARK ZONE

If you've enjoyed your visit into Destination Dark Zone, discover more thrilling stories in Susan May's other short story collections Behind Dark Doors and Destination Dark Zone.

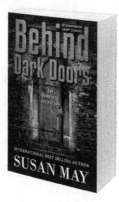

COLLECTIONS

Destination Dark Zone
(COMING APRIL 2019)

Behind Dark Doors (one)
Behind Dark Doors (two)
Behind Dark Doors (three)
Behind Dark Doors (the complete collection)
(Includes one, two and three)

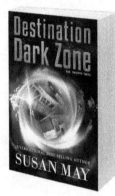

You might also enjoy Destination Dark Zone the soon-to-be-released in July 2019 collection of six dark thriller novellas, which includes Susan May's popular novella 291 (a nod to Stephen King's Christine).

DEAR READER, A FAVOR ...

If you have a spare few minutes, could you please visit the online store from which you purchased **291** and leave a short review (a long one if you like). Reviews help a book gain an audience.

I'd love to hear from you too, so feel free to email me susanmay@node1.com.au or find me on Facebook or Twitter. You will absolutely make this author's day.

STAY IN TOUCH WITH SUSAN MAY

Join Susan May's Ultimate Reader Experience and receive a Susan May starter library of free books.

susanmaywriter.net/free-books

You will receive free stories to keep.

plus

- *Behind the Story* access to fascinating details about the writing of Susan's books.
- Contests to enter with great prizes like Kindle readers and Audible books.
- Free and discounted book offers

- And much more (we're working on the *much more* all the time)

You can find Susan May every day at her private Facebook group **The Mayhem Gang.** You are welcome to join a great bunch of people there from around the world, discussing books, life and other fun topics.

Facebook Susan Mayhem Gang

Connect with Susan May
susanmaywriter.net/free-books
susanmay@nodei.com.au

HAWK EYES & CREW

As always this little book went out to my trusted beta readers, whom I must thank profusely for their never-ending enthusiasm for my work and their crazy ability to spot errors.

I'm convinced these typos and mistakes only appear once I've sent the manuscript to these guys. They sure weren't there when my editor and I scoured the pages.

I like to share part of my book with my early review crew, who kindly provide feedback and reviews. Thank you guys. Here's to all us readers!

Diane & Pete Lynch, John Filar, Dominic, Lagonigro, David Place Jr, Beth Baskett, Bill Schmidt, Mad Wilson, Diane Lybbert, Maureen Scalia, Mike Rice, Shari *USA* Lisa Ensign

I would like to give special thanks to my early review crew who kindly provide feedback and reviews. Thank you guys.

"Wow! Unlike anything I've ever read." *Shari Canada*

"Probably the best novella-length story I've read." *Bill Schmidt USA*

"Another great page-turner from the Mistress of the Twist." John Filar USA

"Could not move 'til I was done." Cathy Weber USA

"Twisted in a good way." David Place Jr.

"Clever premise with an ending to write home about." Retired Bear

"A gripping, fascinating novella." Faouzia

"Huge fan of this author, and this novella did not disappoint." Meghann

"Loved the twist, as always." Dominic Lagonigro

"Could not put it down." Celia Marshall

"Pure Genius!" Lisa Ensign

"The twist in the end was truly fantastic." Tammi Pieczynski

"A horror story with an unexpected ending." J. Phillips

"I just couldn't put this down." Brandy

"Heart-pumping story!" Claudia

"Don't want to stop until you finished the story. "Jillian Johnson

"I know when I read something by Susan May I will be entertained." Christine Lowe

"Better than Stephen King." Concetta Gisone

"So much imagination and creativity." Kandy

"Great characters, exciting plot with a twist." Sharon Leach

"May ratchets up the tension and suspense, leading to a terrifying climax that leaves you gasping for breath." Maureen Ellis

"May's delightfully twisted mind has brought forth another winner." Ian Ness

"This was absolutely amazing." Jane

"Reminiscent of Stephen King's *Christine* or Joe Hill's *NOS4A2*." April

"My mind was absolutely blown by the shocking conclusion." Ami Agner

"Will take you down roads you may not want to explore." Mad Wilson

"You won't dare put this story down until you reach the end!" Beverly Laude

"This is one of the best novellas I have read." Kenneth Lingenfelter

"A first rate novella... a fun read." Camille

"A five star page turner." Nathan Smith

"Susan May just gets better and better. She grabbed me at the beginning and held me to the brilliant twist at the end." Peg McDaniel

From the first sentence to the last "gotcha" at the end, it keeps you guessing." Richard Tamer

"I loved the book. It was hard to stop reading!" Heather Rice

"Where does she come up with this stuff?" Teri

"It was hard to stop reading." Heather Rice

THE TROUBLES KEEPER PREVIEW

Enjoy the opening opening chapters of Susan May's International best selling novel The Troubles Keeper.

HE SAVES OTHERS FROM THEIR TROUBLES. WHO WILL SAVE HIM?

Most of us are lucky if we have one friend to simply be there when we're down. Well, meet bus driver Rory Fine, who possesses the unique gift of relieving others of their troubles. For real! Strangers, friends, anyone he passes by, he can help. With just the barest of touches, for a while, the troubles in their hearts simply fade away.

It's his way of making the world a better place, by giving people the chance to get out from under the weight of their woes. His bus-driving job is perfect because it allows him to meet so many people every day. And all of them are completely unaware why being near him makes them feel happier and more able to face life's struggles.

There's another bonus, too. He's smitten with one of his regulars, sweet Mariana, but he can't find the courage to even say hello. He's shy and awkward and, well, different because of his gift.

Until one stormy night, when he makes a bold announcement to his passengers. Upon disembarking, he suggests they offload their worries into his palm. This might present the perfect chance for him to finally speak to the girl he thinks he just might love.

But...

There's a killer aboard, and he leaves behind something darker and more terrifying than troubles. Soon Rory will discover a powerful entity also seeks Mariana, but his intentions have nothing to do with love.

Can a gentle soul such as he, stand the remotest chance of stopping a cold, relentless evil?

To do so, he'll face more than this enemy. He'll face his own harrowing past. But he will need to find a way to overcome everything he fears. For not only is Mariana in terrible danger but the very fabric of the world is at stake.

From international best selling suspense author Susan May, comes another page-turner keeping readers awake way past their bedtime. Board The Troubles Keeper for a non-stop killer suspense ride. Meet memorable characters you'll love and a world you won't want to leave.

⭐⭐⭐⭐⭐ "Not since Dean Koontz's Odd Thomas have I enjoyed a character as much as I do Rory Fine!" Carolyn Werner

⭐⭐⭐⭐⭐ "Susan May seems to be following in the footsteps of **Stephen King.** I, for one, have already put her on my *'If she writes it, I will read it'* list." Madelon Wilson *(Good Reads Reviewer USA)*

⭐⭐⭐⭐⭐ "A unique take on a serial killer and the author is brilliant at creating a storyline that leaves the reader breathless." Maureen Ellis *(Good Reads reviewer UK)*

Now read the first four chapters of the book readers say they cannot put down ...

The Troubles Keeper

INTERNATIONAL BEST SELLING AUTHOR

SUSAN MAY

1

He examines his work. Certainly not the best he's done but not the worst either. He's improving and becoming more artful. More certain and confident. There's magic in this moment; the *just after* moment when he can breathe again. *In. And out.* A drowning man reaching the surface to suck in pure air so he can survive.

Disappointment rushes in as he feels her last breath. He feels the failure like an ache inside ripping at his core. He felt so certain his search was over, but he was wrong.

He'd found her on the bus. Something had attracted him to *that* bus. Surely the girl, he'd thought. He'd sat behind her as they had traveled downtown. Pretending he'd dropped something, he'd leaned forward. In the closeness he smelled her hair like a bee smells nectar. Sweet. Enticing.

After the bus ride she'd met a friend. A girl just like her, unsuspecting and unaware. As she'd touched her friend, greeting her with a kiss, *there* was the glow, the shine of what lay beneath, inside, where only he could reach down.

At the cinema she was merely four rows away when he saw the shine. Surrounding her, glowing in the dark, a gentle halo of gold as she leaned to her friend to whisper something. They'd laughed, before returning their attention to shared popcorn and the film.

From the multiplex he'd followed, watching from a distance from doorways and shop fronts, pretending to peer into windows. She'd shouted a goodbye to the other—her final goodbye. She hadn't known, so certain there will always be just one more. Does anyone ever recognize their last of anything?

All hope is gone as she slumps. One leg stretched before her, the other bent back beneath the chair like a mannequin awaiting display. Moments before her hands gripped the chair's arms like claws. Now they lay unfurled and limp.

Blood flows in rivulets from the thin, white line carved in her forehead. Red against shiny white bone and pale, translucent skin. Shimmer-black hair falls about her face; strands caught in the blood. He considers brushing them aside to examine the incision, but he's lost his taste for her. He doesn't like the way the face muscles have slackened and her skin droops; how the eyes lay open, staring at him. Above those windows to the soul, white muscle and bone shine through.

As he studies his work he sees his mistake. The hole above her brows, slightly off center, not neat enough. Wrong. Or perhaps not wide enough. The pink-beige flecks of brain matter mingle with the blood. Wrong. The incision is also too deep.

Her fault.

She'd moved, even after he'd explained—in detail, always in detail—why she should be still. Usually they listened. Sometimes not. His concentration had wavered and allowed her to move. He grew stronger with each one though, and soon his control would be absolute and he wouldn't need to bind them.

A long sigh escapes his lips. The need remains, tearing again at him like a climax almost there, but fades away. He wanted, *so wanted* for this to be The One.

He sighs again. No matter, he tells himself—even though this does matter—The One is in this city somewhere out there. He senses her like a hum in the air.

He leans over her, the girl he thought, hoped, would open the door to home. From her brow, he wipes a drip of blood, which hangs like dew. Squeezing and smoothing the blood between his fingertips he thinks back to the bus ride. Something is there behind the curtain of his mind. A strange, little catching lingers, scratching at his awareness, crawling into his subconscious, seeking a memory, a very distant memory.

Now hovering there before him.

The redheaded bus driver.

Could this really be him?

What an ironic twist.

Maybe, *maybe,* this one now just blood and bone and empty flesh, is a sign, a glowing flashing marker. Not The One, but fate's message sent for him. He rolls the idea around inside his mind like the last peppermint in a packet, to be savored, considered.

In that slippery, sliding moment, his disappointment begins to heal. If the bus driver has appeared at this moment, this very day, then there *is* a reason. All he needs to discover is why. He'll take his time. He'll watch. Surely the reason will be revealed.

Reasons usually do.

2

You could blame what happened on the weather.

If not for the sizzling and humid summer evening, the moisture hanging heavy in the air, clinging to everyone's skin, heralding a storm flying toward us, I might never have done what I did.

Rain or shine, storm or blue skies, everything was all fine by me. The weather might get other people down but never me. I knew better.

"Fine" was a great word.

My wonderful mama used to say: "*Fine* by name—Rory Fine, that is—and *fine* by nature."

She peppered my life with that word from the day I entered this world. Until she drew her last breath, haggard and weary, she still insisted *everything* was fine. Always had been and always would be, no matter how much Adversity knocked at her door she wouldn't allow those bad thoughts in.

According to her, my manners were fine enough for the President, should he ever come to visit. My friends, my quite average school results, my smile, my sandy, red hair—the butt of schoolyard jokes—

my stories, everything, was just fine. Nothing earned her reproach. Nada.

"You're the finest thing in my life," she'd say.

"And you're the finest in mine," I'd reply.

The day she left this earth was certainly Heaven's finest and the saddest day I'll ever live. Her last words, spoken in broken syllables and wisps of sound to me, her sobbing seventeen-year-old who'd kept vigil by her bed hoping for a miracle.

"Don't ... cry, my darling boy. God smiled the day you were born. Have a *fine* life my son. That is your destiny."

She may have revised her prediction if she'd known about this hell-hot day that awaited, nine years down the road. There was too much of what St. Alban folk call the Madness Air. The kind of hot that never helps anyone's mood. Or troubles.

A slight breeze blew in off the Dawson River, trying for all it was worth to cool things down just a little. Without that freshening whisper people'd be crawling up the walls by nightfall. Three days straight the heat had invaded our city and sure made my job all that much harder. At the end of a day, all the passengers wanted was to get to their air-conditioned or fan-cooled homes. You know how people look when they've had enough, their muscles stretched beyond capacity and energy on low flow? Well, this described my passengers today. Every single one of them.

I've been driving buses for five years now. A peculiar job for a young man, I know. I know. At twenty-six I should be exploring the world, making my mark, building some kind of résumé to show I've done something with my life and secured my future.

For me though, this job is perfect fitting like a glove with my other more important work. *Life Job*, as I think of my sideline business.

Probably what I do is a smaller scale version of solving global warming by switching off a single light bulb one lamp at a time. So a big job. *Big*. Yet, one by one, I switched off those bulbs, because who knew the effect that might have? Think of my intervention as saving one butterfly that might flap its wings in Bangkok and, in flapping those little wings averts a bushfire in Australia and saves a town. You know the Butterfly Effect, right? That's me, the Butterfly Effect guy. Except, I call this thing I do troubles keeping, which makes me a Troubles Keeper.

I love this job, both jobs, most days. Looking for greener pastures doesn't enter my mind. Even if those thoughts did, I couldn't leave, because in the last six months all had changed. I simply can't leave until everything plays out.

3

Mariana entered my life via the bus's front boarding steps. She delicately boarded the bus, gliding like a dream. Her smile, followed by a casual "hello," hit me like an electric spark that traveled up my spine and charged my soul. Think those zap things that restart hearts. Her smile did that to me. *Smile. Spark. Zap.* Now I'm magnetized to her. *Nope, I can't leave now.*

I'm in glorious, wonderful, very fine love.

The day she hit me with that warm smile was cold, wet, and nasty; not a day you'd expect love to come a knocking. She climbed aboard my bus, soaked and bedraggled, golden-blonde coils, dark with moisture, poking out from beneath her raincoat hood.

Mariana pushed back the hood of her green-with-pink roses patterned coat, looked down her front, then back at me.

"Sorry. I'm dripping. Raining crazy out there. Am I okay?"

Droplets ran down her jacket to puddle on the charcoal-colored steps as she stared at me through running-mascara-blackened eyes. A gentle, magical light switched on instantly brightening that cloud-darkened day.

I heard my Mama's voice whisper in my ear. *Rory, she's the finest, most beautiful natural woman in the world. I like her. I know Mama, me too.*

I remember that day like yesterday, remember I'd wanted to say something smart, something flirty and light. Normally I'm good with a quip. Witty Fine, some call me. Something happened to my brain or my heart or whatever had joyfully twisted inside my chest. My voice had been suddenly held hostage so the best I had managed was a nod toward the back of the bus and a limp smile.

"Thank you," she'd said, pulling and pushing at her coat as though removing a layer of skin. More drops flew about her. Then she had moved down the aisle, her coat now over her arm. The last glance I had snatched in my mirror was of her seating herself next to Mr. Ogilvy (gray-haired, weary eyes and always missing his son).

Six months ago that had happened and still I hadn't worked up anything close to enough courage to squeak more than a "hello" or "have a nice day." I guess that's why today I became bold and took a risk. On reflection, what possessed me?

Love. Unexpressed love.

On this stifling day, air sticky with invisible moisture, the highlight was my anticipation of Mariana's stop. Nearly two years now, the nine-zero-five was my regular route, traveling through City Central with its towering buildings, bustle of shops and department stores, clutter of lunch bars and cafes, and thousands of workers navigating the streets, seemingly always in a rush. From the city we enjoyed a picturesque two-mile drive along the wide and glistening-blue Dawson River, the focal point of the city. Then, on to East Village (doesn't every city have an East Village?). Here we passed the ramshackle, no-longer-in-use, ancient cemetery. Then along Ellsworth Road, the epicenter of the village, dotted with small boutiques, sweet, fine eateries nestled beneath low-rise residential apartment blocks, (sprung up like well-watered saplings since the reinvigoration of the area).

The route terminated at East Village train station by Benedict House, so named to conceal the building was really a halfway house for addicts on the mend. Then the route reversed back the same way.

Three hours after I'd swung the bus out the gates, I drove back into the depot for a break, before repeating the journey all over again.

What most people would consider a mundane job—same streets, same view, same stops and starts—I enlivened by getting to know my regulars. In fact, I did more than get to know them, more than transport them from A to B. I helped them. I changed lives.

They never understood, of course, why on the odd occasion their commute left them happier, more content than when they'd boarded. Maybe they thought the change in mood was due to my friendly smile, or the chance to relax while someone else drove, or that anywhere was better than where they'd just left.

But the difference was me. My touch. My gift to them, delivered without a trace, without a sound, without anybody knowing why suddenly the world seemed a brighter place; the troubles they carried when they left their homes that morning now not so heavy.

I didn't need a thank you or to leave a florist's calling card: *Here's a gift because I can, because I want to make the world a better place.* I didn't need acknowledgment; all I needed were their smiles, their improved moods, and to see extra bounce in their steps as though they no longer toted that emotional backpack.

Troubles. They stick to skin like glue, like gum to the sole of a shoe. They slide into the crevices of your heart, slither into your veins, and tug at you from the inside until they become something dark and heavy and not so easy to shake.

The length of time you allow them to take up residence, that's what makes all the difference between the good, the bad, and the ugly days. Sure, you can brush them aside—and most good folk usually do—but what gets you is the sometimes; the sometimes when shrugging off troubles may not be so simple.

I took away the sometimes.

Dawson River was my favorite stretch. Some days the word *fine* just wasn't enough. The sun rising, yellow and pink, a present to those awake, and the sun setting over glistening water, warm gold, a splendid vista that made you believe in all things good. Some days the river didn't need the sun to shine. Rain splashing its surface,

urged small white-tipped waves to rise up like dancing handker-
chiefs. I knew this river like a friend. We shared a secret; in fact, we
were allies.

This five-fourteen afternoon run was my favorite. Not just
because of Mariana, either. My best work was done in these hours. If
people ever needed relief from their troubles, the time was after a
hard day's work. But, for whatever reason on that day, most passengers seemed to feel the weight of life more than usual. I guess that's
why I did what I did, before I'd thought the whole thing through.

4

He peers through the bus window at the ominous clouds. The light drops of rain, quickly turn the gray of the sidewalk to a mottled black. He likes this dark brand of sky. People are less aware, far more concerned with getting to shelter, staying dry, worrying about plans made more difficult by the heavens spilling down.

Though he walks freely among them, beside these scurrying creatures of habit, there's always a risk he'll be recognized for his true self. Rain feels like an invisible cloak; the humidity like soft, protective fiber against his skin.

Until he found *him* on this bus in the late afternoon, he had spent the day traveling the bus routes, attempting to ascertain if what he felt yesterday was because of this bus, or this man, or a random connection to something else. *Now he knows.* He'd moved seats numerous times, reached out and brushed a few of those around him. *Nothing.* Just a nagging frustration growing within that he may have been mistaken.

Now as he watches him—yes, and the man *is* him—he understands like a faded memory reinvigorated by an old song or the whiff of an intangible scent. He *knows* his search is over.

With each stop he studies the driver, cobbles his memories together, and wonders why he hadn't sought him out before. Of course, he may help him to open the door. *Friend or enemy, though?*

The way he looks at the girl, all golden hair and a smile, as she climbs aboard and skims past the driver, reveals so much. This makes perfect sense; the two of them special lights in a world filled with half-opened doorways and empty rooms. They are both of the same design.

As she maneuvers down the aisle, the girl places a hand on the seat back in front of him. He reaches out nonchalantly to touch her. Electric fire, blue and sharp, rushes through his skin.

She could be The One.

He soaks in this knowledge, and the peace this thought brings. This long search could be over. Her brow lifts playfully as she looks down at his hand; surprise crosses her face. He smiles and withdraws the hand, feigning embarrassment. She smiles. Unsuspecting. No reason to fear. A random accident of physicality, a moving bus, an unbalanced body.

Now she is his and he can source her at will. A thrill plays through him and goosebumps rise on his skin. For the next fifteen minutes he slides between exhilaration and frustration that he must wait until tonight. He'll follow, but he's learned through experience that timing is everything.

Then the bus stops and the driver stands facing down the aisle. He introduces himself. *Rory Fine.* Has the man recognized him? Surely the bus driver cannot know or he would have noticed a reaction.

As the bus driver talks he begins to understand. This isn't a random chance meeting that he is here on this bus with her. Something grander is at play. He just needs to figure out exactly what that means.

Continue reading
for FREE with Kindle Unlimited or Kindle Prime

The Troubles Keeper

Available also in whisper-synched audible

The Troubles Keeper

ALSO BY SUSAN MAY

NOVELS

The Goodbye Giver (THE TROUBLES KEEPER 2)

(COMING LATE 2019)

Best Seller

The Troubles Keeper

Deadly Messengers

Back Again

NOVELLA

291

Behind the Fire

OMNIBUS

Happy Nightmares! Thriller Omnibus

SHORT STORY COLLECTIONS

Destination Dark Zone

(COMING JULY 2019)

Behind Dark Doors (one)

Behind Dark Doors (two)

Behind Dark Doors (three)

Behind Dark Doors (the complete collection)

(Includes one, two and three)

WHISPERSYNC AUDIBLE NARRATION

291

(COMING JUNE 2019)

Destination Dark Zone 2019

(COMING AUGUST 2019)

Best Seller

The Troubles Keeper

Deadly Messengers

Back Again

291

BY SUSAN MAY

Copyright © 2019 by Susan May

All rights reserved.

THE TROUBLES KEEPER

BY SUSAN MAY

Copyright © 2016 by Susan May

All rights reserved.

The stories in this book are fiction. Any resemblance to any person, living or dead; to any place, past or present; or to any thing, animal, vegetable, or mineral; is purely coincidental.

However I'm quite the people watcher, so if you have crossed my path I may have stolen some particular quirk from you for a character. It means you're memorable.

CPSIA information can be obtained
at www.ICGtesting.com
Printed in the USA
LVHW031834160719
624281LV00006B/895/P

9 781796 784107